Larry Cabaldon
Brian Klemmer

D1165122

GOD IN THE
BOARDROOM

why is Christianity losing market share?

GOD IN THE BOARDROOM
why is Christianity losing market share?

Published by PCG Legacy, a division of Pilot Communications Group,
Inc. 317 Appaloosa Trail Woodway, TX 76712

Printed in the United States of America
with The Publishing Hub

ISBN: 978-1-936417-14-8

Contact the authors:

Larry Cabaldon
www.boardroomperformancegroup.com

Brian Klemmer
www.klemmer.com

"For where two or three gather in my name,
there am I with them."

— Matthew 18:20 (NIV)

Contents

1

The Emergency
Board Meeting

The voices were indistinguishable behind the two massive, ornately carved wooden doors. People were greeting one another and talking loudly in order to be heard. One voice boomed, and the room went quiet. After a while, the noise seemed to pick up again behind the closed doors.

It was 9:15 a.m. Barry Smith, boardroom coach and consultant, had been asked by the assistant to the Chairman of the Board to meet the board members at 9:00 a.m. As usual, boards are never on time.

The reception area was traditional dark paneled wood with a huge granite fireplace, intricate wood moldings, deep patterned carpets with walls covered with plaques and portraits of the Chairman and the CEO. Barry reached across the classic coffee table for his cup and saucer, stirring in the sugar with a silver spoon. *Forbes*, the *Wall Street Journal*, *Architecture* magazine, *Above Rome* and an ancient, thick Bible were spread out neatly on the table.

The receptionist, an attractive, gray-haired woman who obviously took charge of the room, was talking to the security guard/limo driver about travel schedules. "Need more coffee?" she asked.

Barry shook his head and said, "No thanks," then started to fiddle with his Blackberry. He mumbled to himself, "Maybe I should get a Twitter account, but even if people were following me, they wouldn't believe who my clients were."

He put his Blackberry on silent mode and took one more sip of the warm coffee. He could be called in at any moment.

As Barry sat in the large leather chair, he recalled the many times He had waited to meet and present to the dozens of boards of directors because their organizations were in trouble. He reminisced about past successes in keeping boards from going under. He felt confident in his ability to make positive changes, though this assignment would be different than the rest.

The noise subsided in the boardroom. That powerful voice spoke again. Then one of the massive doors opened and the Chairman's assistant stepped out and said, "The board is ready for you now."

2

Why Is Christianity Losing Market Share?

The boardroom was large, all of it a polished dark walnut color. The floors were of dark green marble. The table in the center seemed to be cut from one massive tree, and it sat solidly in the middle as the center-piece. It was wide enough to fit three chairs at each end, and a dozen or more on each size.

As Barry walked into the room, he quickly scanned the faces. There were about thirty people around the table, all of whom were obviously top-level leaders. At the head of the table were only two chairs. From one of them stood a powerful looking man who politely welcomed Barry.

"Thank you for joining us on such short notice," he said. "Please take a seat for now. I want you to hear a presentation, then I will officially introduce you to everyone here."

Barry thanked him and sat in one of the smaller chairs against the wall. From his vantage point, Barry studied each face, remembering all that he had learned about these leaders.

It was then that Barry noticed the Chairman, seated beside the CEO, was wearing a robe. "I've done work for churches, universities, and ministries," thought Barry to himself, "but I've never seen a Chairman wear a robe."

The Chairman spoke directly in a way that commanded respect. If anyone could wear a robe, he could. He definitely was the leader, and like an ancient king, he evoked fear and respect. He also had a cutting sense of humor that he would use at times to both challenge and direct. It was a strong combination.

The CEO seemed less aggressive and confrontational, yet he also had an aura of great power, but with a gentleness and wisdom that seemed to shine through.

The Chairman bellowed, "Thank you all for coming. I know you are all busy super-achievers. I want to congratulate each of you for your success on the behalf of the company. You have brought in many customers and subscribers and have done a lot for our community image in helping the poor, the sick, the downtrodden, and those with spiritual emptiness. You have been successful in your areas of influence. My Son and I," he motioned to the CEO, "want to thank you and express our personal gratitude for your efforts. We know it's tough. However, with that said, I am not happy."

He paused there for dramatic emphasis. Barry glanced around the room. The leaders were nervous. They were fidgeting. One was chewing his nails. Most had a determined, yet sad look on their faces, like they had struck out at bat, leaving the bases loaded.

The Chairman continued, "Despite your best efforts in your own organizations, we are losing market share faster than ever. Keep this up and the company could go under. I'm going to ask my Son to give you the report."

His Son stood up and the room darkened slightly as the projector buzzed in the silent room. The first slide showed a simple figure:

32%

The CEO looked around the room, then he began, "We are thirty-two percent market share in the global market. In ten years, some studies show that Islam, because of demographics and other issues, will surpass us. People are not using our product correctly. They often start out right, then try the 'do it yourself approach,' like they do at Home Depot. The key issue is this: We are losing in our mission to dominate the marketplace. That is our key mission."

One of the members raised his hand. You could tell he was itching to say something. After getting a nod from the CEO, he stood up and was about to speak when the Chairman cut in, "I know what you are going to say… That you question the statistic, that you want further research done, that we shouldn't even discuss percentages, and that not all the information is on the table. Well, you are correct in one way, but the point is not the actual number. The point is the downward slide. Nobody can question that."

"And while we are mentioning statistics," the Chairman continued, with a noticeable tone of impatient anger in his voice, "who can explain the fact that more than half of all marriages end in divorce; that the USA alone has aborted millions of babies in the past few decades — I could give you the exact number, but I won't — and this number continues to mount; drug use and crime are rising; and your TV stations keep lowering their supposed standards?"

The board member closed his mouth and sat down. There would be no more outbursts from him, and nobody else was moving either. They were all quiet, hoping the Chairman's questions were not meant to be answered.

The CEO cleared his throat, then presented other charts that showed losses in the developed countries, young people, attendance at events, and more, all to emphasize his point.

"Here is the bottom line," he said. "How can we not question the value of all that you do if we have such a downturn across the board?"

As the members weighed the meaning of those words, the Chairman interrupted again. "Pardon my frankness, but it seems that some of you are so busy cannibalizing market share among yourselves that you are not even aware of the situation around you. What is the problem? You are my key people on earth who have been given all necessary authority. You swore to uphold our mission and vision, and yet you are not performing!"

More fidgeting, more shuffling of papers. This meeting was hot!

The CEO continued, "The second part of our mission is customer satisfaction. We are supposed to treat customers as we would like to be treated. That is what attracts and keeps customers. According to our surveys, our customers are not using our product or following our training. For example, let us look at moral metrics — metrics that support our way of products, services and values."

Across the screen flashed many statistics about poverty, crime, drugs, abortion, divorce, AIDS, orphans, promiscuity, unwanted pregnancies, abuse, depression, suicide, prisons, and more.

Glancing briefly at the still-red member who had spoken up about wanting more information, the CEO said, "Again, it's not the exact percentages or the exact numbers. You are failing to provide the benefits of our products and services as evidenced by your results. You are losing minds and souls. You, my trusted executives, are losing market share and not delivering the value we all have promised."

The Chairman sat forward in his chair. He had everyone's attention; there was no need to stand up. "What are you doing?" he asked bluntly. "How could you, as the spiritual leaders that you are, mess this up so badly? We have already given you the manual. Supposedly, you know what we want and how to do it… So what is the problem?"

The room was completely silent. No shifting around in the cushioned chairs. No pencils scratching or keys clicking. Those around the table and those around the walls were conscientious enough to know that they had failed in their given responsibilities. Nobody stepped forward with an explanation, much less raised a hand to ask a question.

It was an embarrassing moment for the members. Their silence simply confirmed their guilt.

As the Chairman sat back in his chair, the CEO stated, "That is why we have asked Barry to join us," motioning for Barry to come to the front. "He is going to assess our company, our key leaders, and our businesses and come up with hard-core recommendations for change. I expect one hundred percent honesty as you cooperate fully with him."

He continued talking as Barry walked forward, "But Barry isn't going to be the only one doing the hard work, the research, the questioning, and the number crunching. You are going to do it with him."

Usually Barry was the one who did the digging and prying, then reporting and recommending, but the CEO was right. The results would create greater buy-in and more support — not to mention the fact that these leaders could then train their personnel more easily from what they learned themselves.

The CEO went on, "I'm giving you thirty days to answer the Chairman's single question: 'Why are we losing market share?' I want you to come up with your own answers. Do research in your own cities and in your own areas of influence. If that takes you to people you would not normally speak with, then so be it. We expect a full report from each of you. Remember, each of you must meet with Barry during the next thirty days. Then exactly forty days from today we will all meet back here."

The members were taking notes as fast as they could. They were all paying close attention. That was a good sign for Barry.

"I don't want there to be any questions, any excuses later," the CEO explained, quite patiently. "Do you understand your assignment?"

Everyone nodded.

"Good, then please gather your things and exit through that doorway," he motioned. "There is something we need to do together."

3

Revealing Intentions

The Chairman stayed seated as the members slipped quietly out of the room. The CEO caught up to Barry as he was heading toward the door, "Barry, I want you to take everyone through the IMR game that I've seen you do all the time. It's necessary here."

"Okay, I'll do that," Barry responded. Barry loved the game, not only because it was fun to play, but because of the changes that took place in people's minds as they played it.

The side room that they entered was bright and spacious. It was a large break room, with coffee and tea along one wall, several chairs and tables, and then a whiteboard at the other end. In the middle was an open area about twenty feet long and thirty feet wide.

"I've asked Barry to do a little training with you," the CEO explained. As all eyes looked at Barry, he could sense their relief. They were glad the spanking was over.

Barry began, "Let me start by telling you a little about my background. I consult to boards and management teams who are in crisis. I have helped boardroom teams uncover the issues and take committed action. As to the reason for our coming together, I have my own questions and doubts, so I hope to learn a lot from you as we go on this journey together. We must get to the truth. I look forward to getting to know you individually over the next thirty days, so let's dive right in. You all know James 2:17, correct?"

The soundman already had the verse in several different translations and it flashed up on the whiteboard:

- In the same way, faith by itself, if it is not accompanied by action, is dead. (NIV)

- So you see, faith by itself isn't enough. Unless it produces good deeds, it is dead and useless. (NLT)

- Even so faith, if it hath not works, is dead, being alone. (KJV)

- In the same way, faith by itself is dead if it doesn't cause you to do any good things. (GOD'S WORD TRANSLATION)

Barry read the verses out loud, not because they couldn't read, but because he wanted them to focus on the task at hand.

"Now, I need everyone to move to the right side of the room," he explained. The CEO was smiling as he leaned against the back wall.

Barry continued, "This game is called the IMR game. It stands for Intention + Mechanism = Results game. You are familiar with this concept from Proverbs 23:7, which says that 'as a man thinketh in his heart so is he.' Well, many times we read or listen to a sermon and it goes

16

into our head or conscious mind, but the heart or subconscious is not changed. Is that not frustrating?"

Several of the leaders looked at each other and nodded their heads knowingly.

"It may sound a little strange," Barry stated, "but I've learned that we can play certain games that will effectively take head knowledge and turn it into a change of heart. Let's begin with some definitions, which are viewpoints or belief systems, and I'll give you the definitions so we are all operating from the same place. In this game, we are going to define Intention as *your deepest commitment*, Mechanism as the *how to*, and Result as *what you get*."

Barry took a second to write the three words and their definitions on the white board.

"Most people have a goal, and then they brainstorm a mechanism as to how to make the goal happen. That's fine, and it works well — for a season — but that is a conscious mind or worldly approach. To be a faith person, you have to be 'out of your mind,'" he said with a chuckle. "Let's play this game and see what revelations you have."

Ignoring the blank stares, Barry explained, "I want each of you to cross to the other side of the room using a unique mechanism — or simply put, get across in a different way."

One member took off walking. "Very good, but too easy," Barry said, positioning himself near the center of the room. "Let's see what each of you comes up with."

The next few included crawling, spinning, waltzing, hopping, and running. After everyone had successfully crossed the room with a unique mechanism, Barry asked them to continue the exercise and go back the other way with yet a new mechanism. A few murmurs and complaints were audible as people struggled to come up with a new mechanism.

Suddenly, a woman, Pastor Joan, took off quacking and flying like a duck trying to avoid a dozen hunters.

Everyone started laughing. Barry stepped in, "You see that? She might look pretty silly — and indeed she is — but she did what most of you wouldn't do, and she got the results she wanted."

That seemed to bring in a fresh wave of creativity, and soon all the leaders made it across the room again.

"Now, let's do it again," Barry exclaimed loudly, "and this time everyone must use a unique mechanism and no one can use your legs!"

The shock on their faces was evident. They were bewildered. The guy who had walked across first had the biggest eyes of all.

"I don't know any way across the room," he spouted, showing some frustration.

"Perfect!" Barry replied. "This is exactly the experience you have when you don't know what to do to get your staff aligned behind your vision… or you don't know what to do to double the size of your church… or you don't know what to do to raise five million for a missions project or church building with the size congregation you have… or you just cut your staff (lost the use of your legs) and you still must get the job done."

As the man stood there, looking at Barry, another member started rolling across the room. The man said, "No, I really don't know what to do. That was very creative, but that must be the only way to do it without legs."

Barry calmly pulled out his wallet and held up a hundred dollar bill. "For one hundred big ones," he said with a smile, "I bet you'll come up with a new way of doing it, but I am only giving you thirty seconds to come up with a mechanism with no legs to get across, and you can't roll."

The man was immediately on the floor, doing a sidestroke swim to get across! Everyone laughed, and then clapped, as he reached the other side to collect his hundred. Within minutes, every person had made it to the other side with a unique mechanism and without using their legs.

"Did you see what happened?" Barry asked. "As I understand, the Bible tells us that *'with God all things are possible.'* I believe that means we have all the creativity we need. God has blessed us with options beyond our current understanding, but it is our human nature to try to solve things with our conscious minds. When you say, 'I don't know what to do,' all you are saying is that your conscious mind doesn't know what to do. However, your subconscious has plenty of options…and with God you have an unlimited number of options.

"So the challenge is to access your subconscious mind and to reach God to solve problems rather than using your conscious mind," Barry went on. "That is a faith message. We will talk about how that process just worked in a moment, but let's hear what revelations you have just had."

Barry took a breath and looked at the thirty now-friendly faces as their hands shot up in the air with their insights. An older man said, "I am astounded at the infinite number of mechanisms for just one intention — to get to the other side. I will admit that I have been operating out of scarcity for many years and that there were only one or two ways to get members to stay engaged in our church after they have visited."

Another leader eagerly pointed out, "I got it. When Joan flew across the room like a duck, I was thinking to myself, 'I would never look foolish like that,' and that's my congregation. Their intention or deepest commitment is to not look foolish to their friends, so the fact they want to evangelize is irrelevant. They don't actually want to bring visitors to church."

"I guess as a pastor," spoke up one young man, "I have to ask if my intention is to give a great sermon, impress my peers, and motivate people to support my latest program … or am I really doing this to serve God and equip His people?"

"Those are tough questions to ask and answer," noted Barry, "but it is important that you do just that."

Another board member excitedly shared, "When Joe came up with the sidestroke so quickly to get the hundred dollars, I saw how when my intention is clear, a mechanism appears seemingly out of nowhere. But it is God responding to my commitment and faith. I guess I need to focus on intention rather than on the mechanism, since there are so many. Focusing on my deepest commitment or intention instead of brainstorming mechanisms will actually produce a mechanism."

"That is an outstanding insight," Barry replied. "Let me summarize the IMR. The real formula is Intention = Result one hundred percent of the time, without exception. Intention without results really isn't intention. Faith without works really is dead…or really isn't faith."

One of the members questioned, "So, as an example, you are saying that if we run a meeting and the result is that we haven't gotten anything done, then it wasn't our intention to get anything done?"

"Exactly!" Barry said. "You and others certainly wanted to get something done, but you had a deeper commitment to something else, like to be in control of the meeting or to not hurt someone's feelings by bringing up a sensitive issue. Remember, intention is not what you want or a target or what you plan on happening. It is your deepest commitment."

He continued, "So you must question your intention if you are not getting the results you want. Awareness is the first step toward change. If the systems you are using are not working today, then you need to change something. There are easier ways across the room than others, but the bigger issue is that it wasn't your deepest commitment to get that result. Be open to challenging your beliefs. Be open to changing or redefining your intentions, and be open to coming up with new mechanisms to get the results you need instead of being stuck in the belief that there is only one way to do something."

Someone asked from the back of the room, "What do I do if I am not getting the results I want? Change my intention so I do get the result I know God wants me to have?"

"Now you are thinking!" Barry exclaimed, clapping his hands together. "Since intention is the deepest commitment, you must raise the commitment to what you want higher than any other conflicting commitment. There are four ways to do that."

Barry turned toward the white board as the members grabbed their pens and papers in unison. He wrote:

- Clarify your real intention

- Make promises

- Put yourself at risk

- Visualization

"These are like chemical ingredients that activate God and your subconscious to get involved," Barry explained.

Many of their faces showed the lights were coming on. Barry could see it happening around the room as several heads nodded in agreement. He turned back to the board and continued writing:

- Question intention if I'm not getting the results I want.

- Awareness is the first step toward change.

- Remember there are infinite mechanisms for any intention.

- Make a promise and put yourself at risk to activate faith and create a mechanism.

"Thank you, Barry," the CEO said, as he stepped quietly to the front. "And thank you all. Joan, good job on quacking across the room. And Joe, that legless swim was priceless. You all learned a lot of valuable lessons that I want you to take with you as you work during the next thirty days as you meet with Barry and as we move forward together."

As if on cue, Barry started handing out business cards to everyone, knowing that he would be meeting primarily with these leaders who had sat around the table. "Please call or email me about when is good to meet, whether it's over the phone or face to face," he explained. "We will need to meet, including your key people, for a few hours. I will want to know what you are doing and why, including all your intentions, mechanisms, and results."

The CEO, looking around the room of leaders, added, "We are also very interested in what you find out on your own. That, along with Barry's assessment, is what we will discuss when we meet here again in forty days. Remember, the question to answer is this: 'Why is Christianity losing market share?' Now, go figure out what's going wrong."

With that, the meeting was over. A back door opened, which led to the foyer, and all the members exited.

It was then that Barry saw the Chairman, sitting at one of the tables. Barry walked over, but didn't sit down. The Chairman seemed lost in his thoughts for several seconds. Then he stated, "Did I not send my Son to be sacrificed for their sins? He took a gentler approach — focusing on love and not fear, respect and not wrath — but I'm wondering if a stronger combination of the Old and New Testament is needed. Tough love! I sure hope the leaders who sat around this very table can figure this out."

Barry had to ask the CEO, "Why did you and the Chairman pick me? There are more experienced consultants with more knowledge of the Bible. I've had conflicts over the Bible and disagreements with pastors over their leadership and interpretation of the Bible and leading of people. I am not the strongest of believers. I'm a sinner and I am by no means perfect. I think I'm a regular guy with doubts and cynical questions."

The CEO spoke, "Barry, we don't pick perfect people. Moses killed a man and was not a great leader. Noah, Jonah, David, Abraham, and Sara, they all had doubts and weaknesses. That's why we picked them. We want to always transform the person who accepts the challenge. You represent the average person who has doubts and questions, and that is why we chose you. Because of that, you will question and challenge the thinking of these leaders."

It made sense to Barry, logically, but he felt very unworthy.

"Remember the disciples," the CEO continued. "After three years of working with me, seeing my miracles and teachings, they rejected me. They only returned when I came back, resurrected. What kind of faith does that take? In a similar way, this will be a test for you, for the leaders, and for all of mankind. This isn't based only on you."

Barry was humbled and awestruck. But he realized, too, that he had to be courageous in doing his job and not back down from the board members who were smarter, more powerful, more educated, and more committed than him. This was going to be a major challenge. Was he up to it?

Barry responded, "I'll do all I can to help."

With that, the Chairman and CEO walked out. The door clicked closed. Barry was alone. The next month would indeed be interesting!

4

Are Christian Leaders Asking the Right Questions?

As Barry parked his car in one of the pastor's covered parking spaces, he couldn't help but feel as if he were at a vacation destination like Disneyland or Sea World. The asphalt parking lot was several football fields in length, in every direction, and the church and other office buildings were so large that it seemed logical that they were renting office space to businesses in the community.

People with Bibles, posters, and notebooks were scurrying around with enthusiasm and excitement. Barry saw several cars lined up and people dropping off bags of donated clothes and food. There were rows of custom painted vans and buses lined up by one of the buildings, obviously the K-12 school that was so often in the news.

Barry asked one fast-moving young man with jeans and a black t-shirt where he could find Pastor Joe. The young man cheerfully escorted Barry to the church office.

"Mrs. C, someone to see Joe," he said, then slapped Barry on the back and skipped out the door. Barry moved across the tiled floor to be a bit closer to the receptionist and out of the steady stream of people walking in and out of the door.

"Is Pastor Joe expecting you?" she asked.

"Yes," Barry replied, and then added, "We were in the same board meeting last week."

Her eyebrows went up a bit as she searched through her working schedule for Pastor Joe.

The receptionist tapped her earpiece and then spoke, "Rachel, someone is here to meet with Pastor Joe. Can you come down and take care of him?"

The church phone system was constantly beeping, so the separate phone line and earpiece for the pastor's office was probably a necessity.

Within seconds, Rachel appeared. She was college-age, pretty, and outgoing. "Come on up," she said. "I'll take you to Pastor Joe. He is just finishing up in another meeting."

Barry followed her up two flights of stairs and into a second office area where another receptionist was busy on the phone. Rachel led him through a doorway into a large conference room. Boxes of printed materials, DVDs, and VBS coloring books were scattered about. There was a large white board filled with diagrams of organizational flow charts and red arrows and circles.

"He'll be done in a minute. Can I get you a Coke, coffee, or water?" Rachel asked, like a perfect hostess.

"A water would be great, thanks," Barry replied.

Alone for the first time, Barry noticed the two huge bookcases against the wall were filled with the latest Christian books, self-help, pop psychology, history, motivation, US history, sports heroes, and famous biographies. One shelf, upon closer inspection, was filled with books they had published under their own publishing label. Above the shelves was a PowerPoint electronic pull down screen. The conference phone sat in the middle of the large table.

The minutes ticked by. Barry was about to ask Rachel what the delay was when she popped her head in the door and apologized, "Sorry for the wait. Pastor Joe was in a staff meeting, but is ready to see you now."

She led the way down another hallway to the pastor's office. It was more impressive than most CEOs Barry had worked with. Paneling, thick rugs, pictures with celebrities, including the Pope, Presidents, sports figures, and politicians, adorned the walls and credenza. Certificates of appreciation, mugs, and souvenirs from Africa and India, plus golf clubs, were scattered around the room. This was an office as well as a showroom.

Pastor Joe stood up and shook hands. He remembered Barry from the game they had played after the boardroom meeting, and the fact that Joe had won the hundred dollars. He chuckled, "That was a funny game you had us play," as he motioned for Barry to sit down.

Barry laughed as well. He knew Joe liked being the center of attention, and for a minute in the game, he was ... and the hundred was a nice perk. Barry hoped Joe had learned the lesson.

Joe said, "Let's begin with a prayer," and after a quick prayer, he jumped in by asking who Barry knew that he knew, about Barry's background, which church he attended, what he did do to serve the Lord, and finally if Barry knew what Pastor Joe had accomplished for the Kingdom.

All the questions were designed to place Barry in the proper Christian pecking order. In his many interviews with CEOs, he understood the drill, so he didn't let himself get excited or defensive. He knew that once they actually got around to dealing with the Chairman's directive, all these questions and views by Pastor Joe wouldn't really matter that much.

Pastor Joe paused, and Barry sensed he was satisfied with the answers he had received. "I know your time is valuable," Barry stated, "so let's start. First, I need to clarify any questions you may have about our assignment. What is your understanding?"

"Right," Joe said with enthusiasm, sitting forward in his chair. "Our Chairman is rightfully concerned about the overall condition of Christianity and wants us to examine what can be improved. Well, let me tell you what we've done to make improvements. We get it. I wrote a book on this subject. We understand that other churches are stuck in the past, so we looked at what's not working in our market and decided to make major changes in our music, sermons, and outreach to make our church relevant and significant to today's seeker."

Barry was jotting down notes as Joe pointed out one of his windows, "Look at our campus. Exciting, isn't it? Just walk around and you'll see the changes. Come to our services and you'll feel the energy and entertainment value we provide while maintaining our commitment to the core Biblical principles. Have you come to any of our five weekend services?"

"Yes, I came to one of your conferences several years back," Barry explained.

"You're a business guy," Joe continued. "I just left our staff meeting. All of our key metrics are up. Attendance, small groups, mission trips, outreach programs, support guys, baptisms, and offerings. We are expanding! We have fifty percent penetration in our market and we're growing in every direction."

He continued, "I am supportive of this study because the other churches must get with the program that we've so successfully implemented. I've been trying to tell the Chairman and CEO this for years.

God in the Boardroom

We're doing great! Just look at our numbers. I firmly believe we need to set a great vision in place and then have faith in God and the people to execute it. If others in the boardroom were to follow our formula for success, we'd get that thirty-two percent market share number up in no time. I'm convinced. It's worked for us."

"Congratulation on your achievements," Barry said, looking up from his notes. "I'm interested in knowing a bit more about your experience and journey. Can you tell me about how you got here?"

Pastor Joe related his journey from humble beginnings as a child in a hard-working farming family. "I wanted to go into business, but ended up in the seminary," he noted. "After I graduated with my doctorate, my vision for church growth expanded and God guided me and helped me make it happen."

By "it" Barry understood Joe to mean that he had reached the coveted mega-church level. Barry made a few more notes, not about his story or church, but about the pastor himself:

- Proud of achievements
- Thanks God to try to remain humble
- Competitive
- Believes he has God's special blessing
- A probable control freak
- Stuck in his own bubble

Barry asked, "How successful have you been at retaining members? You know, keeping the people who come in the doors of your church."

"Well," he began, "the school has almost a one hundred percent retention rate, and the waiting list is a mile long. Our sports and science programs are stellar, and I'm sure they are helping keep our numbers up. Our outreach programs that feed and clothe the poor are always looking for more donations as the number of needy just seems to grow exponentially."

He was starting with the best and working his way down the list. Barry had expected it.

"The church and our related programs are constantly growing, with more and more people coming. As I said earlier, our numbers are only up. Take our youth ministry, for example — we have several new buildings, two new youth pastors, and several rock music concerts and service projects planned for our community."

Barry wondered if Joe ever did have a problem; if so, would he even be aware of it? Pastor Joe was Mr. Positive with God's backing.

Probing a little deeper, Barry asked, "What is the commitment level within your church — with those on staff and those who serve in some area of responsibility?"

"Our staff are one hundred percent committed," Joe replied quickly. "The same applies to our other leaders within the church. They are fully on board, committed, and hard working."

Barry was about to ask another question, but Joe continued, "A few months ago, we let one youth leader go. I don't think he shared my vision, and I knew it was a test, so I let him go. We all have to be on the same page to accomplish things."

Outwardly, Pastor Joe was nothing but positive, but Barry's questions seemed to be putting Joe on the defensive, so Barry decided it was time to get into the details of his assignment.

"Here is the assignment we have for you," Barry explained, handing Joe a single white piece of paper of questions. "As you know, the primary directive from the Chairman is why Christianity is losing market share.

To answer this question, we want you to ask questions such as these: 'Why did you leave the church? What improvements should Christianity make to attract, retain, and expand Christians?' We want you to ask these questions only to those who have left the church."

As Joe skimmed through the questions, Barry added, "I will take your findings and synthesize them with other data for our boardroom report at the forty day mark, so I need your report within the next two weeks."

"In addition," Barry said as he stood up, "In your role as a consultant to the board, please remove your pastor hat. Be open, non-judgmental, and listen for the truth and feelings from each interviewee. Do you have any questions?"

Barry didn't expect any questions. Pastor Joe only had answers.

"No problem," Joe replied. "I counsel many people, so I know how to handle this type of interview. I'll keep them in line and get this info back to you right away."

Afraid that he might simply delegate this task to a college intern, Barry warned, "Pastor, you need to do this research yourself. You need to be the one who asks the questions. And remember, your job is to gather information and feelings so that we can understand the issues, so be very careful not to defend, argue, preach, or lead the interviewee to your conclusions. Can you do that?"

"Sure."

"Very good," Barry said, hoping this would indeed work out. "Thank you for your participation and cooperation. I look forward to your findings. Call me if you have any questions."

As Barry walked out of his office, Rachel met him and led the way back down the stairs and to the front door. Barry waved to Mrs. C., who was speaking into her earpiece, and headed to his car.

Barry sensed a familiar pattern. Strong, dedicated leaders like Pastor Joe who were self-confident because of their own successes were also usually blinded to any other option or perception. Their supreme confidence in their own vision and ability to persevere despite any obstacles was precisely why they are so successful. However, Barry knew these powerful qualities made for leaders who didn't react very well to crisis or change.

Barry had to trust that Pastor Joe wouldn't be so focused on his strengths and past successes that he would fail to hear the answers to his own questions. On top of it all, Barry had learned many years ago that mixing God with strong leaders and strong visions could result in even more obstinate leaders. It was always a risk.

When Barry got back to his car, he turned on the air conditioner and pulled out his notes. Looking at the schedule, he had similar meetings on the books with the other spiritual leaders who had sat around the boardroom table. One pastor happened to be speaking at a college commencement in a nearby town, so Barry would get him later in the evening.

Barry wondered to himself, "Will they listen? Will they learn? Will they be transformed so they can see the real issues and react appropriately?"

From past experiences, Barry knew transformation was possible as people saw things differently, listened to others, and experienced the pain of not changing. Barry believed their brief training on intention, mechanism, and results would also help.

Change was always possible, and he hoped all the leaders would find real answers for the Chairman. If not, he also knew that leaders who do not change in a crisis would eventually have change forced upon them.

5

.

Why Is the Church Losing Young Warriors?

Pastor Joe was not looking forward to interviewing people who had left the church. "I don't think this is a good idea, or a good use of my time," he whispered to himself. But before he had too much time to think about it, one of his enthusiastic staff members sent out an inter-office email that Halden Mack, a twenty-five-year-old man who had left the church several years ago, was back from Iraq. He had been wounded on his second tour and was at the local Veteran's hospital.

"Okay, I'll go," Pastor Joe said, after reading the email. Because of his mega-church vision and world travels, Joe had stopped doing funerals, weddings, and hospital visitations himself, but because it was the Chairman's directive, he went ahead and set up the appointment with Halden.

The next day, the driver dropped Joe off at the hospital entrance. As he was signing in, he saw Halden's mother, Marge, walking his way. "Hi,

Pastor Joe. I heard you were coming, and I am just leaving, so I'll walk you in."

Joe was relieved to have help. Walking aimlessly down hospital hallways was never fun, and the hospital smell always turned his stomach.

"How is he?" Joe asked.

"Oh, he's doing much better, thank you. And thank you for coming," she added, "it means a lot to us."

"So, what happened to Halden?" Joe inquired. "Maybe I can get the story from you, as he's probably too humble to tell me what he really did over there."

Marge smiled in agreement. "I'll tell you the short version. He was ambushed by a group of insurgents. He suffered major internal injuries when he stepped on a landmine on a dirt path between two suspicious buildings and was blown ten feet into the air. Five courageous buddies pulled him from the smoke and sniper fire to safety, and within forty-eight hours he was transported by Humvee to a waiting C-17 that flew him to Germany, London, New York, and then here. He has been recuperating for three months."

Pastor Joe remembered that Halden had attended church all the way from VBS, through the teen trotters club, and the fireside fellowship programs. When he started at the community college, he attended church less frequently, and then he volunteered for the Marines. Since then, he hadn't been back to church.

As they walked through the halls, they saw many young men in wheelchairs and walkers, or walking with IV tubes hooked up to poles on wheels. There were families, friends, girlfriends, wives, and military chaplains everywhere. They did not recognize Pastor Joe because he wore nothing to identify him as a man of the cloth. Traditional robes and white collars were considered old fashioned and authoritarian to his market segment. He chose to wear blue jeans and a polo shirt, but despite that, he felt uncomfortable and powerless in these surroundings. Remembering that he was the pastor of a ten thousand member church helped give him confidence.

"He's out in the garden atrium," Marge was saying. Halden was basking in the sun, stretched out in his wheelchair, looking like a surfer relaxing in a chaise lounge after a morning of surfing with his Oakley sunglasses and iPod.

Marge tapped Halden on the shoulder, and he pulled out his earpieces.

"Hi, Hal, remember me?" asked Joe.

Hal looked up and removed his glasses. His eyes were bloodshot and tired, but he slowly acknowledged and respectfully greeted Pastor Joe. His military training served him well.

"I'll be back this afternoon," Marge said with a pat on Joe's shoulder, and then she walked back inside.

Joe and Halden exchanged pleasantries and talked about Halden's little brother, who was one of the star football players in the church's school program. After a short pause, Joe pulled a lawn chair closer to Halden and sat down, saying, "You know, God works in mysterious ways, and there must be reason for what has happened to you. I believe that we need to have faith in God and that everything will work out. After all, God is in control, and He's watching over you. You may not realize it now, with all the pain and suffering, but this is a test of your faith."

Hal had listened politely, but now he held up his hand, "Time out, preacher."

Pastor Joe was silent. Nobody talked to him that way, and he would give Halden a few minutes to make things right before he would head back to the office.

"I admit that I was not a strong Christian at church," Halden began, "but when I got into combat in Iraq, I discovered a strange fellowship with my fellow soldiers. We all feared dying, seeing our friends killed, or having to kill an enemy. Because of that fear, we turned to Jesus Christ. No matter the denomination or interest in Christianity, we considered Jesus to be the answer."

Joe was processing, and listening.

"We desperately wanted Jesus in the Humvee, on our night watches, in the helicopter, and on patrol because we knew anything could happen to anyone at any time," Halden said with emotion. "However, and you need to hear this part ... the soldiers rejected institutional religion. They felt that churches were irrelevant, and I agreed. Churches here in America are more about the pastor than about Jesus."

Now Joe was really listening.

"We survived because we were realistic, not because we were naïve, happy, or pretending. The truth is, death is the best evangelizer because it challenges your beliefs to the very core of your foundation. For me, it created a unique personal bond with Jesus, my Savior."

Joe didn't want to interrupt. What Halden was saying should be preached from the pulpit!

Halden spoke softly, yet firmly, "We carried Bibles. We prayed together. We didn't chitchat about Christian stuff. Instead, we had genuine fellowship and connection to Jesus Christ, and we connected with each other on that same deep level."

"I hear there are many different types of chaplains in the military," asked Pastor Joe. "What were they like?"

"Honestly, a chaplain can't help you when you're on the front lines. It's between you and Jesus at that point." After a second, Halden continued, "Things are so politically correct. Many times it's all about respect and tolerance rather than about getting your heart right with God. In the old days, we fought for God, country, and family. Now, they want to take God out of the picture, and it doesn't work. No offense, but in many ways, the chaplains are as ineffective as the preachers back home."

Pastor Joe looked intently at Halden. "I'm not offended," he said honestly. "I think I understand what you are saying. I really do."

Halden was tired but relieved that he had spoken his mind. Those feelings and emotions had been bubbling up for years, and it was good for him to finally tell a pastor, his pastor, the cold hard truth.

"Will you regain the use of your legs?" Pastor Joe asked, with a new sense of compassion.

"The doctors have me in this wheelchair mostly for my internal injuries, but my legs should be good eventually. My left foot is gone, but the prosthetic one works, and I'll survive." Halden put out his hand, "Thanks for asking."

"You know," said Pastor Joe, shaking Halden's hand firmly and rising to go, "It would be a real honor to have you speak some weekend at church. We have five services, and I wouldn't ask you to speak in all of them, but if you spoke in one of them, I know you would pack the house. It would be great to hear your heart and to hear about Jesus being so real in the trenches."

"If you're serious," Halden said with a laugh, "I think I would like that. Thank you."

"No, thank *you*," Joe said. He turned and walked back toward the nearest doorway. Sniffing away a tear, he thought to himself, "Wow, where have I been? How many other Haldens are out there?"

The ride back to the office was quiet. Pastor Joe turned off his cell phone and used the fifteen minute drive to make several pages of notes.

6

Is the Church Connecting with the Marketplace?

Bishop Mike liked his small suburban church, but what pleased him the most was that he had recently been given responsibility over twenty-five other churches in a three-state area. These other churches were small or medium size, and by adding them together, he calculated his total reach to be around 12,500 people. This was good news, for he wanted to climb the denominational ladder as far as he could.

Even before he went to seminary, Bishop Mike liked being the man in charge, the man in front. He longed to be in control, and seminary was a powerful way to expand his intellect. It provided him with the training and collar to brand himself as a man of God. He used his power and opportunity to interweave his political and social beliefs into his sermons. It's what he did, and he liked it.

The small church was Mike's fourth appointment. The first had been temporary, the second a few years, and the third was to have been more permanent, but internal strife within the church had scuttled his plans.

When this new vacancy appeared, Mike turned on his charm to connect with the older, conservative congregation as well as with the youth and young married couples. This made the search committee happy, and a few weeks later, Mike had a new church and was hard at work.

"Bishop Mike," Barry said when he called, "Congratulations on your appointment over so many churches. I imagine you are going to be speaking a lot."

Mike replied, "Yes, that's what I really love to do, so I'm looking forward to it. But I don't think I can help too much with the Chairman's request to find out why we are losing market share."

"Oh, really? And why is that?" Barry asked, a bit surprised that Bishop Mike would be so quick to drop his responsibility.

"Well, as you may also know, I'm new at this church, and don't feel I have adequately created a sufficient relationship with its members to be able to provide you with the necessary data for your survey."

Barry couldn't help but notice the use of larger words and the preparedness of Mike's refusal. "Thank you for your concern," Barry replied, glad that he had done his homework in advance on this one, "but I was aware that this was your fourth church and that you had left your last church under some disagreeable terms. Because of that, I think you are in the perfect position to gather the 'necessary data.'"

"You do, do you?" Bishop Mike asked, himself a bit surprised.

"Yes, and here's my thinking on that," Barry explained. "I would like you to interview one or two couples who left your last church or who were instrumental in you leaving the church."

There was a long pause, and then a cough, as Bishop Mike tried to formulate a reply. "Whoever said that ignoring an issue never really makes it go away was right on the mark," muttered Bishop Mike, mostly to himself. "I just wish going back and dealing with people and issues from the past wasn't so hard, stressful, and even painful."

Up until this point, Barry was really wondering if Mike would be of any help, but the honesty of his answer was encouraging.

"Well, it will be awkward, I'll grant you that," Barry responded with compassion, "but I'm sure that good will come of it. Can you set up an appointment with one or two couples in the next few weeks?"

"Actually, I'm heading back there in just a few days to collect the rest of my things, so it's certainly doable," Mike answered. "In addition, there aren't one or two couples — there is only one couple, and they live near my old church, so I'm sure I can arrange it."

"I know you probably don't want to," Barry admitted, "but thank you for doing it. Let me know how it goes, okay?"

With that, Barry hung up and Mike was left to follow up on his promise. "Why am I doing this?" he grumbled, "I did promise I would try, but I can't guarantee that it will happen."

Mike dialed a number that was still programmed in his phone. Immediately, he heard a "Hello?" at the other end.

"John, this is Mike," he began a little hesitatingly, "I will be back in town in a couple days ... would you, uh, have time to get together and talk for a bit?"

"Sure, I can do that. Call me when you are here."

For the second time, Mike was left holding the phone. "I hope this is worth it," he exclaimed, slowly letting out his breath.

After driving for almost nine hours, Bishop Mike pulled into his old hometown. The memories were still fresh, as was the pain. He had called John an hour earlier and had arranged to meet in the corner of

Mama Cita's, Mike's old favorite Mexican restaurant. It was mid afternoon, so the place would be almost empty.

As Mike pulled into the parking lot, which was shared by the restaurant and a fitness club next door, he scanned the cars for John's beloved black BMW. When he saw it, parked near the back, he felt his stomach tighten up. "Here we go," he muttered.

Gathering up a pad of paper, a pen, and the questions that Barry had emailed him, Mike walked around the front and up the short steps to the door. All the while, John was watching Mike through the side windows.

John Carrington, at age fifty-nine, was a few years older than Mike, but had lived here his entire life. He and his wife, Helen, were married by their favorite pastor, the very pastor who had retired and whom Mike had replaced.

Their old pastor sincerely cared about everyone. John remembered how he, Helen, and their pastor had spent time together, working through issues. Both had been married before and had many questions and hurts, which made their pastor's non-judgmental friendship and counseling so healing. He remembered their pastor saying one day over coffee, "It isn't about you being perfect; it's about God being perfect. He loves you more than you will ever fathom, so as you seek Him, deal with issues as they come up, but know that God is on your side."

Those words meant a lot to John, and after he and Helen were married, they became active members in the church. John, who had a knack for investments in all things real estate, was able to help many people in the church. And as a result, the church experienced increase in giving, attendance, mission work, and more. It was a really special time, and John loved walking in peace in the gifts that God had given him. He and Helen grew a lot during those twenty-one years, both in their marriage and in their walk with God.

When Mike came, things began to change. He didn't know John or Helen, which was understandable, but the fact that he discounted John's ideas and suggestions to help those within the church and within the community began to take their toll. Being part of the church's work wasn't quite as enjoyable after that.

"Just give him some time," said Helen, who was ever patient, but in time, Mike seemed to grow more judgmental, more anti-capitalist, and more liberal in his viewpoints. At a Christmas party, Bishop Mike cornered John and began to hit him with questions: "Are you really doing enough for the Kingdom? Are you tithing? Are you over focused on making money? If you would focus more on giving rather than exploiting, the world would be a better place."

John had put down his drink. He had served the church in many ways, spending countless hours and much of his own money, beyond his tithe, with special building projects, helping families in the church who had lost their jobs, and helping others make wise investments with their money.

"Pardon me," John had replied, trying to hold back his anger, "in all I do, I am serving, trying to create value in others, and working ethically. If you are hung up on the tithe, I'd say it's a bad tip! I give more than ten percent to the waitress, and I give more to the church as well. Why don't you focus on helping people expand their ninety percent rather than criticizing them for being productive with it?"

From that point forward, John had felt that Mike was trying to get him to leave. When John and Helen's oldest daughter gave birth, Bishop Mike had refused to do the baby dedication, claiming it was the result of John being unfaithful with his tithes. This hurt Helen tremendously, and she had wanted to leave, but John tried to mend the rift by multiple voice mails, emails, and attempts at setting up a meeting.

The final straw came when John waited in line to shake Bishop Mike's hand after church one day. When it was John's turn, Mike had completely ignored him, moving right past John to the next person.

Helen had been watching and waiting, and when she saw what happened, she had burst into tears. That was it, and neither John nor Helen ever went back to Mike's church.

In time, John and Helen found fellowship and new friends at another church, but the hurt was still there. The issue had never been resolved.

"Hello, John," Mike said as he walked up to the table. John was brought back to the present in a flash. He stood up and put out his hand. "Good to see you, Mike. Have a seat."

Mike laid his papers down, with the questions on top. "The reason I'm here," he explained, "is that I've been asked to follow up and ask you some specific questions."

"Okay, go ahead," John replied. He had expected Mike to skip any pleasantries and to get right down to business. "I was surprised that after four years you would want to bring up this issue, but I'm glad you have. Who else is involved?"

After ordering his favorites off the menu, Mike replied, "I've been asked to gather some data about couples that have left the church, and you and Helen were the one couple that came to mind."

"There were others who left after we did," John replied.

"Yes, that's true, but I didn't know them very well at all," Mike responded. "But in addition to you leaving, I must admit that you were part of the reason that I left the church."

John tipped his head questioningly, "Really? That was years ago when we left. And what did I ever do to make you leave?"

"You questioned my authority," Mike answered, "and what hurt even more was the fact that everyone in church loved and respected you. There were so many who had been helped by you, and these individuals never really listened to me again after you left. I would say that about ten families and individuals left within the year, and I know that most were because of you."

"Wow, I didn't know that," John replied. He and Helen had made it a point to leave the church quietly and to never bad-mouth Mike to anyone. "But I didn't question your authority in front of you or anyone. Sure, I disagreed with some of the things you said, but it wasn't me against you."

"This is supposed to be about why you left the church," Mike stated, trying to bring this discussion back into focus. "So, tell me, why did you leave the church?" Mike asked.

"Well, I never expected you to ask, but since you are, I'll tell you," John said, sitting forward at the table. "First, you never seemed to really care about people. I saw how you were charming, articulate, and funny with the search committee, but they wanted to be convinced. I noticed how the young people were impressed with the fact that you knew the names of the rock bands, how the older people appreciated your knowledge of history and your apparent conservative ways, and how young couples were impressed with your understanding of problems of raising kids and pressure, even though you've never been married. Do you still wear that Jack Daniels tee shirt? You were so open to all faiths, but inside, you really didn't seem to care about anyone."

Mike was trying to take notes and listen at the same time. Part of him wanted to slap John for being so offensive, but deep down inside, the accuracy of John's words was almost frightening.

"In one of the meetings, I remember you said that it would take you three to five years to get the church the way you thought it should be and that you did not mind people leaving who did not fit your profile. You actually said that! I couldn't believe it, because to me, you were telling people right to their faces that they should leave if they didn't agree with you."

"Anything else?" Mike asked, glancing up quickly as he took a sip of his drink. He was sweating.

John nodded. "Yes, actually there is, and this one took the longest for me to see and understand. The my-way-or-the-plank routine was easy to notice, but what really started causing confusion and questions for Helen and me was what you were preaching instead of preaching Jesus and His Word. Week after week, it was all about your liberal beliefs and your politically correct position on things."

"Give me some examples," Mike sputtered, trying to keep his questions, and John's whole grilling, as objective as possible.

"One great example was one of your favorite hot button speeches about a woman's right to choose," John stated. "I want to know how anyone could say that it's okay as a nation to kill over 3,500 babies per day. I did the simple math by reading reports that we've killed approximately forty million babies since we legalized abortion. That means the total number of soldiers killed in the war in Iraq is about equal to the number of babies we are killing on a daily basis. Come on, under what circumstances is that acceptable, for any nation?"

Mike shifted his feet.

"And how many times did you try to convince us that homosexuality was okay and was supported by the Scripture?" John went on. "I know the church's governing body has been arguing over this issue for years, but you manipulated the congregation into moving towards your viewpoint."

Taking a breath, John continued, "I lost track of how many times you criticized people, businesses, and our soldiers overseas. You were quick to jump on any business scandal, but you never criticized those who had no money, who cheated on welfare, or who lied on applications. You mocked those who were productive, caring, and responsible, and you praised those who cheated and stole. What does that have to do with teaching the Bible?" John asked passionately.

Mike wasn't writing any more. He was staring at his questions on the table.

John continued, a bit more quietly, "In fact, based on your sermons, I really started reading the Bible more carefully myself and researching various interpretations so that I wouldn't rely on anyone else's interpretation to run my life. So, I guess I should thank you for that."

Mike wasn't sure if he should take that as a compliment or not.

"I want a pastor who helps me know God more and who inspires me to bring the practical values of Christ into the world," John explained. "It's not about being righteous, opinionated, and critical. That describes the Pharisees in Jesus' day, and they were the very ones who killed Him."

Mike was trying to take notes, but he was hardly paying attention to what he was writing.

"Mike, isn't a liberal supposed to be open minded?" John asked with sincerity. "I mean that, I really do. I know you are well read on business, leadership, economics, political issues, and the like, but you don't really seem to be looking for the truth."

Bishop Mike had to restrain himself. He believed firmly in his liberal philosophies. How dare this uneducated man lecture him!

"Can you be a bit more specific?" Mike said through clenched teeth. Finding his breath, and the next question on the list, he added, "Actually, what can I do to improve?"

John sat back, feeling better that he had gotten the burden off his chest, but doubtful that the conversation would have a happy ending. "Let me ask you a question," he said. "Would it be better to help families create money and work jobs so they can live with dignity, or would it be best to go on giving them money, knowing that only a small percentage of them will ever try to get a real job?"

"I can see the importance of 'creating value,' as you call it," Mike admitted with a bit of sarcasm, "but the church's job is to help the poor."

"I totally agree with you — we have to do both," John said with a smile. "I find that my giftings allow me to help the first group, and as the Bishop, you handle the second group. I do believe, however, that we should aim for the first group more, but not neglect the second group. If we only serve the poor by giving them money, we are not helping their dignity or creating value. We are, in fact, damning the lot of them to a life of welfare and mere subsistence. That is certainly not a life of abundance."

It was Mike's turn to agree. "You know, as much as I don't want to, I must admit that I am in agreement with your logic," he replied, feeling a sense of peace in his situation. "I have never really considered why I don't want to accept such thinking. Perhaps it isn't your logic that should concern me, but rather my desire to not agree with you that should be my point of focus."

"I'm not meaning to overstep my bounds," John empathized.

"No, I realize that," Mike replied, "I think I need to hear it. The result of me not listening to you, and pretty much cutting you off, meant that when you left my church, we lost a portion of our ability to provide value, dignity, and work for those who so desperately needed it."

The men looked at each other, and Mike put out his hand, "I'm sorry for the pain I caused you and Helen, for not listening to you, and for the loss that your absence brought to the church."

John smiled, shook Mike's hand firmly, and stated, "I forgive you. I'm sorry, too, for the losses we all have experienced."

After a pause, Mike said, "I will tell you that I don't necessarily understand or agree with everything you've said, but I recognize that I have not even tried to listen to you, and others, over the years. I promise to at least consider your points for what they are without immediately shutting them out."

"I couldn't ask for anything more," John said, amazed that Mike, one of the proudest and most egotistical pastors he had ever met, would say such a thing.

"Ignoring things doesn't make them go away, does it?" asked Mike, knowing the answer to his own question. "That has been my approach for years. I wouldn't listen, and then if something did happen that was contrary to my beliefs, I would ignore it. I'm learning something."

"And what is that?" John asked, as a friend would.

"That the truth will set you free," Mike replied with a chuckle. "And that peace follows right behind truth."

John nodded approvingly, "Well said. I like that."

"Well, John," Mike said, holding up his glass as if he were making a toast, "let me make a promise to you. Though I may never see you again, I promise to seek truth, to keep my heart and ears open, and to truly be a servant to the people in my church."

Their glasses clinked together. Wounds were healed. A friendship had been restored. The future was changing for both men.

Mike added, "Thank you, John, for telling me what I needed to hear, even though you and I both knew that I didn't want to hear it. I can't tell you how much it means to me."

"Likewise," John replied. "Helen will be begging me for all the details before I get home, but it's a story that I won't mind repeating."

They rose to go, shaking hands once more.

John left the parking lot, speaking to Helen on his cell phone, and Mike sat for a few minutes in his car before he sent Barry a short text message: "You were right."

7

Protecting the Children

The archbishop was busy, extremely busy, but he had a habit of remembering small details. He knew that his turn would come. Ever since the board meeting with the Chairman and CEO, he knew that he would be getting a call from "the Barry fellow" in regards to the research they were supposed to be doing. The archbishop was too busy to stop, listen, and answer irrelevant questions, much less do the required research. He hoped, not too secretly, that Barry would somehow get sidetracked along the way.

Tuesday morning, the phone rang at 8:00 a.m. sharp. A few seconds later, the phone on the archbishop's desk buzzed. "Sir, a Barry is on line one for you."

Since pretending to be occupied would only prolong the matter, he picked up the phone and jumped right in. "Barry, how are you? What can I do for you?"

"Well, sir, good morning," Barry replied, ready for the down-to-business approach. "The plan, as you know, is to work with a select number of leaders from the board meeting and help them gather the necessary data for the upcoming meeting in two weeks. What I need you to do is look through your list of parishioners who have left the church and set up an appointment with one of them. Then through interviewing that person, we hope that you can find answers to why the church is losing market share."

The archbishop smiled to himself. He may still get out of it yet. "The problem is," he explained, "we have no way of tracking parishioners through our multiple churches. Some leave because they have moved away, others visit only for holidays, and some have left but because of some unknown reason. Whatever the reason, we really have no way of tracking the comings and goings of our parishioners."

"That's totally understandable," Barry responded. "I have a better idea. Have you lost any good priests over the past few years?"

Without thinking, the archbishop blurted out, "Yes, a very good priest, Father Jack, left a few years ago. I don't remember why he left, though we did talk about some street protestors or something like that. But I have no idea where he has gone."

"Good choice," Barry said. "See if one of your assistants can track him down. Let me know what you learn."

Before he hung up the phone, the archbishop had resigned himself to not getting much done that day. Surprisingly, it only took five minutes for Father Jack to be located.

Father Jack was quite surprised to receive a call from the archbishop's office requesting an appointment. He was asked, or told, that the archbishop would be arriving at 10:00 a.m. the following morning and that Jack should be ready to address certain issues about leaving the church.

"Discuss the reasons why I left the church?" Jack said to himself with a slight chuckle. "That's going to be a long meeting."

.

As he thought about it, his mind went back to that fateful day, five years ago, when something snapped inside of him. He had been driving to the church for a meeting when he took a turn through Surf City. He hadn't been there in several years. Before he had become a priest, he used to surf, buy his wax from the local surf shop, down beers at the Main Street bar on Saturday night, and eat a late breakfast on the street tables watching sixty-year-olds on their Harleys, gorgeous California girls on bikes, and hot cars cruising Main Street.

When he had turned the corner on Beach Boulevard towards Huntington Beach and Main Street, he saw the usual carnival atmosphere: tourists from Japan buying t-shirts, skateboarders snaking their way through the crowd, trucks with advertising banners for Cuervo Gold, and a mixture of surfers, want-to-be surfers, and tourists all enjoying the beautiful California day and the excitement of crossing at Main and Pacific Coast Highway. In the background, loud rock music emanated from the surfing contest arenas and tents on the beach.

Father Jack had noticed some extra commotion, cars honking, placards on poles, and people lining up along the sidewalk. He saw several signs supporting the legalization of marijuana, but the focus was on the well-organized signs lined up like Roman poles. Father Jack looked closely and was shocked to read the signs: "Jesus says don't kill babies!" "Jesus will turn on you!" and "Judgment Day is coming!" The crowd was reacting like an insulted mob.

Father Jack had been offended and embarrassed by this display. Everything about their behavior supported all the anti-Christian stereotypes: self-righteous, insulting, and an in-your-face attitude. It seemed that most of those passing by were angry, and they taunted the placard holders, who in turn responded by quoting scripture verses. The result was a strong anti-Christian mood.

Father Jack had been outraged. He worked hard to change the stereotypes and reach out to young people and overcome their perception that Christians were guilt-ridden, self-righteous, in-your-face bigots and replace it with real love and acceptance.

He had pulled into a nearby gas station, knowing that the few minutes he parked there would not get him towed, and walked directly up to one of the placard holders who was in a heated argument with a passing motorist. He had interrupted, "What are you trying to accomplish? I bet any Christians walking by today are embarrassed and probably wouldn't admit that they are members of the same religion. What are you doing?"

The young man had said, "Just trying to share the Word, sir. Our leader told us to expect resistance and persecution. He was right. We just need to intensify our efforts for Christ and not waiver in our commitments."

Jack had replied, "Do you really think what you're doing is good for Christianity? Or is this just some self-centered, self-righteous display for your own ego or purposes? Do you like the feeling of being persecuted by taunting the crowd? Do you really think you attract people to Christ? How can you call yourself a Christian? Where is God's love? Where is God's forgiveness? You are going to destroy all the hard work by real Christians!"

The placard holder didn't have a verse to fire back in defense, but Jack was already heading to his car.

Fifteen minutes later, still in a huff and late, Father Jack had entered the massive, ornate cathedral. The weekly staff meeting of thirty other priests had already started. The archbishop gave Jack the "admonishing look" when he slipped into the room like a freshman late for class interrupting the dean's pontificating lecture.

The archbishop had spoken of the love of Christ, the evils of sin, the truth, acceptance, tolerance, and righteous rage over sin. Twenty-five minutes later, he moved on to the administrative details. "We need to encourage business men to tithe to the maximum," he said. "Call them on the greed and unwillingness to share. Recount the corporate scandals and cover-ups as evidence of their group sinfulness. We need to preach to divorced women on adultery, the sin of fornication, and the fact that Jesus is the only way to heaven."

Jack was trying hard to stay focused. "I should have grabbed a coffee," he thought to himself. "I knew I would be late anyway."

"Most of all," the archbishop had said, "we are called to remind all people of their unworthiness, wretchedness, that they can do nothing without Christ, and that the church is the only way to grow spiritually, be held accountable, and serve the Kingdom. All must support the church regardless of their economic status."

"I can't believe those guys out there with their signs!" Jack had found himself thinking. "Those obnoxious, self-serving, placard-carrying Jesus freaks, how could they use Christ for their own purposes? How could they use the Lord to beat up on people?"

"Our messages must be dramatic, compelling, and action oriented," continued the archbishop. "The archdiocese needs money, because the tithes, membership, donations, and support are down significantly since the priest pedophile scandals and the highly publicized lawsuits and investigations."

"What are they trying to accomplish by what they are doing?" Jack had wondered. "Do they really think this helps people, brings them closer to Christ, or expresses His love? Yelling at people and demanding that they change or be damned to hell is not going to fix anything. How could it?"

Suddenly, Father Jack had been struck by a lightning flash of insight and awareness. "We are doing the same thing!" he blurted out.

The archbishop had stopped speaking. His eyes came to rest on the perpetrator, "What was that, Father Jack? Something you would like to add?"

"Uh, no. I'm sorry," Jack had mumbled, embarrassed that he had interrupted the eminence and that everyone was looking at him. Then he said, "I didn't mean to interrupt. I understand what you are saying in a whole new way today, thank you."

The archbishop had smiled in reply, and the meeting continued.

"Oh my goodness!" Jack had thought to himself, "The archbishop is telling us to do exactly the same thing the Jesus freaks are doing. Our meeting is in a big cathedral, we are well educated, ordained men of God, and the message is more subtle and godly, but it's the exact same message! We are saying, 'In the name of Jesus Christ, we want you to do X (pay tithes, do this, do that), and if you don't, you'll go to hell.' What kind of Jesus are we preaching?"

Father Jack was never the same after that Saturday revelation. He began to question himself and other priests. The word "Pharisee" kept coming up, which he felt aptly defined those who use religious rules, protocol, and power to control others to do their will. After a passionate sermon came a call to action that usually served the church's need or vision rather than the Lord directly.

As Jack had wrestled with his own questions, a major scandal involving another pedophile priest and years of cover up by church leaders occurred in his area, involving people he knew and respected. That was the final straw, and Father Jack left the church.

Jack would often sit, watching the sun set, and ask himself, "How could the church, representing Jesus who cared so much for children, cover up such a hideous crime and let more children suffer at the hands of clergy-uniformed monsters? How can I be part of the same church that preached so vehemently against corporate lies and stock manipulation and that perpetrated the largest and out-of-integrity cover up in history?"

He ended up at the same point each time. Logically, the cover up made sense, for survival is the strongest motivation of any individual or group, but it still hurt that he had given so many years and so much effort to the church, only to see it crumble into the dust. "If only the desire to serve the Lord could override our desire for survival," Jack reasoned. "That would be something to be a part of."

Five years went by, and Jack did not return to any position of leadership in any church. He continued to build his personal relationship with Jesus and found a small non-denominational church nearby to attend. He felt called to work with abused children and became the Executive Director of a non-profit that served over two hundred children in Santa Ana, California, a low-income, mainly Hispanic, suburb of Los Angeles. He enjoyed his work and quietly went about his duties with much satisfaction.

"Wow, what a sudden shift," Jack said to himself, breaking into his trip down memory lane.

The next morning, at precisely 10:00 a.m., Jack looked out his small office window to see an entourage descending on the non-profit's small parking lot. The archbishop arrived in a presidential-like large black Tahoe SUV. Out jumped two suits with earpieces who scanned the area, then opened a side door and ushered the archbishop toward the entrance. The security was necessary, Jack knew, for people often acted aggressively when they recognized the archbishop when he traveled.

Jack's young intern-receptionist-assistant was overwhelmed as she excitedly called from her desk in the front, "Jack, you gotta come check this out!"

The archbishop would arrive like a visiting politician, Jack remembered with a grimace. Charming, friendly, but quick to remind all that he held an exalted position. He had the power to give and take things. How he carried himself and spoke were constant reminders of his power.

Jack rolled his eyes as he turned from the window. A few steps later he entered the front office just as the two suits with earpieces closed the entrance doors.

"Hello Jack. It's been a long time. How are you?" said the archbishop, walking toward Jack, his priestly robes swishing with each step.

Jack replied, "Fine, your eminence, and how are you?" remembering all the etiquette he had learned in priesthood.

"I'm getting older and coping with more pressures today," was the archbishop's reply, "but God will guide me. Tell me about this place."

Jack explained, as he led the way back toward his office, "Well, it's a center for abused children who have been orphaned, abandoned, or mentally and physically abused. We provide services, support, and hope for them as they work to rebuild their lives. We have just over two hundred children. Many of them live here in this converted warehouse and motel facility. It was donated by a wealthy orphan and is funded by donations."

The archbishop nodded approvingly.

Stepping into his office, Jack added, "I was inspired by Spencer Tracy's classic movie *Boy's Town* where he played a tough, loving priest who dramatically helped hundreds of boys. I really enjoy serving young people and making a difference in their lives and creating a positive future."

"That's great, Jack. I always knew you had a heart for children," stated the archbishop, as he plopped down in the only chair in Jack's office, "and if I had time, I'd love to tour your facilities, but I'm here quite literally on a mission from God. I've been asked to help on a project supported by other Christian leaders to answer a few rather open-ended questions, such as, 'Why is Christianity losing market share?' and 'Why are people leaving the church?' I'm here to ask you these questions so that we, most importantly, can find out what we can do to regain people for Christ."

Jack was stunned by the questions. He didn't expect questions such as these, much less the honesty by which the questions would need to be answered if they were going to provide any useful feedback. "And you came to see me?" was all he could think of saying.

"Yes, and I need to know why you left us five years ago," the archbishop asked pointedly, pulling out a pen and a pad of paper.

Looking deeply at the archbishop before speaking, Jack asked, "You want me to tell the truth rather than be polite, don't you?"

"That's why I came to you," the archbishop chuckled. "I knew you would say it like it is."

Jack thought about all the sexually abused children he had counseled in this very office, many of whom sat in the same chair the archbishop was sitting in now. "You should hear the stories. They are painful beyond description, and they leave scars that literally last a lifetime," Jack began. "The pattern is frighteningly predictable: adults in a position of trust, be it uncles, brothers in law, scout leaders, teachers, coaches, YMCA counselors, or priests, molest these young kids — not once, but repeatedly! The most despicable are the Christian men who occupy a place of special trust and access."

"Go on," the archbishop replied.

Jack decided to explain his reasoning, "It started with those Jesus freaks on Pacific Coast Highway. You remember — you and I had an email exchange about them and how I challenged them to reconsider whether they were following the Lord or in fact hurting Christianity? Well, in our weekly meeting that Saturday, I realized we of the church were doing the same things, only worse because we had more power and more influence than those Jesus freaks did."

"Explain to me how we, the church, were 'doing the same things,' as you say," asked the archbishop calmly, without showing any sign of anger or impatience.

Taking a breath, Jack plowed forward, "I was extremely shaken when I realized that we were not following the teachings of the Lord and in fact we were using the Bible to justify our sins. I joined the priesthood because I love people and I love the Lord. I wanted to serve both for the glory of God, but when I saw how we used our powerful position to judge and control people through guilt, shame, and righteousness to achieve our own agendas or protect us, I could not in good conscience continue."

Jack continued, "And then when the church chose to protect pedophile priests and allow more molestation of children, I was through! The continued resistance and cover-up was unconscionable to me. How could men of God allow monsters to continue to victimize small, innocent children? And I know I'm pointing my next question to you, but I asked myself, 'What kind of leaders would allow repeat offenders to strike again?' That question left me no choice. I had to leave."

"We aren't here to blame or point fingers," the archbishop stated a bit too forcefully, and then said more evenly, "Please proceed."

Jack found that he didn't care what title or position the archbishop held. This was the only opportunity that Jack would ever have to speak up for the children who needed help. "True, I'm not here to point fingers, but I do not believe we should do what is right as a result of outside pressure. We should do what is right simply because it is the right thing to do, not to mention that it is a moral and spiritual issue as well. No wonder there is hatred in the streets."

"Perhaps," stated the archbishop matter-of-factly, "but there's more to it than that. It's a complicated issue that involves ..."

With a snort of disgust, Jack interrupted, "Oh, it's always more complicated than people will ever understand, but it's only that way because we make it so. I see daily the hideous results of not living our lives according to Scriptures. Are we not committed to God and His teachings? Are we not committed to protecting our young people from threats at this very moment? Honestly, how complicated is that?"

The archbishop was not used to taking notes, much less used to being grilled with questions that addressed both his professional life as well as his personal life. Trying hard to stay on track, he said, "I cannot deny your perception or your pain. You have dealt first-hand with far more betrayal and sexual abuse than I ever have, or ever will."

There was a long pause, but Jack didn't interject. The archbishop seemed to be thinking, lost in his own world.

"How can I, in good conscience, respond to what you've said with an intellectual or legalistic argument?" asked the archbishop. "I feel like a Nazi leader trying to respond to the grandson of a Jewish holocaust victim at a concentration camp burial mount. In light of devastating evidence of pain and suffering, what is my defense?"

Again, Jack didn't say anything. There was nothing to say. He had read the press releases, the legal arguments, and the well-crafted sermons that came from the church, but none of it really addressed the real issue.

"Based on what you've said," stated the archbishop, as he repositioned himself in his chair, "is this why people are leaving the church?"

Jack combed his hair with his fingers and nodded. "It's probably the biggest reason right now. This hypocrisy and cover up has caused many to leave, but it's not just that. People are tired of being preached to and tired of being told, 'Believe what we tell you and do not question the church if you want to go to heaven.' The people are revolting because they want — and must have — their own relationship with God. You, the church, should encourage this rather than discourage it."

"But we have weekly meetings to plan our topics of discussion for all the priests," the archbishop began in defense, then added, "Never mind, that's not the point. What else? Could you be a little more specific?"

Raising his hands with passion, Jack continued, "Being a believer means that you believe the core Gospel truths, not every political, economic, leadership, and psychosocial point that comes from the pulpit. The more church becomes about calls for action and new programs, the more people are going to leave. We need to get back to preaching God's Word and loving people."

"Okay," replied the archbishop with a tint of sarcasm, "What would you suggest we do to improve?"

Taking his Bible from the corner of his desk, Jack flipped to the back and took out a small white piece of paper. "I occasionally jot down my thoughts to this very question," he noted. "Here it is, in bullet form."

The archbishop held the paper in his hands. It read:

To reach the world, we must:
- Listen more
- Live with integrity
- Quit preaching guilt
- Stop being hypocrites
- Eliminate Pharisee thinking
- Show genuine love to all people
- Protect the children
- Be humble, open, and honest
- Speak the truth from God's Word
- Serve

"That's quite a list," commented the archbishop.

Jack agreed, "I started on that list when I first became a priest, and it still motivates me to get up each day to help others. Basically, it's what was preached from the book of James, part of which says, '*This is pure and undefiled religion in the sight of our God and Father, to visit orphans and widows in their distress, and to keep oneself unstained by the world.*' Honestly, your eminence, is the church pure and undefiled?"

"No, we are not," admitted the archbishop, "and I truly wish I could say otherwise."

Closing the Bible, Jack sat up straight in his chair, "By your cover ups, it is my belief that lately the church has done more to destroy Christianity than the devil has."

The archbishop was speechless. No one ever spoke to him so directly and with so much passion, insider perspective, and truth. Of course, he would never give someone a chance to say these things either. Slapping his notebook closed, the archbishop stood and said, "Well, Jack, you've given me a lot to think about today. Thank you. It will help me as I report back to the board."

As they walked out, the halls were full of kids standing in line for lunch. The laughing and talking quieted down a little as the adults walked by. The archbishop couldn't help but look in the eyes of the children. His heart skipped a beat as he realized just why these children were here. Behind each set of young eyes was a story of pain. How much of that pain had he, the archbishop and leader of the church, caused?

The archbishop took a few faltering steps and then stopped. He looked Jack in the eyes and said, "Like you, I was inspired with all my heart, soul, and mind to save the world and to serve God. What happened to me? I feel like I've become this legal spokesperson for the church who spends more time trying to manipulate the press and save the church than in doing what I wanted to do in the first place."

Jack stepped forward and put his arm on the archbishop's shoulder.

"Where is my heart for the Lord?" whispered the archbishop. "Where is my heart for the children? What have I become? And what kind of personal relationship do I have with Jesus Christ?"

As if on cue, more than twenty children gathered around the arch-bishop and laid hands on him and prayed for him, right there in the hallway. A few minutes later, with tears streaming down his face, the archbishop held up his hands and stepped back. He knew he should give each one of the children a hug, but he didn't know if he should.

He didn't know if they would want him to.

One of the older kids, a teenager and a mentor to many of the younger ones, stepped forward and said, "Sir, you don't know me, but I'm called 'Lasso' by everyone here. My real name is Katallasso, which is Greek for ..."

"Yes I know," interrupted the archbishop. "It's Greek for 'reconcilia-tion.' And Lasso, you may know of me, but despite that, would you be willing to give me a hug?"

Without hesitating, Lasso put his arms out and they embraced. It instantly became one massive group hug, with more laughing and tears. Invited by all the children, the archbishop stayed and had lunch. When he left, he felt like he was fifty pounds lighter, though he did look a little disheveled. His robes were crumpled, and there were too many tear marks and food stains to count.

"What happened here today?" asked the archbishop as he and Jack walked back to the front office.

Jack replied, "God happened, your eminence, and it was amazing, was it not?"

"Yes, it was," the archbishop agreed. "I can't put it into words right now, but I will in time. I have much to do, Jack. I have much to do."

With that he turned and walked out the front door, leaving his two suits with earpieces to chase after him.

8

Love Your Wife, Respect Your Husband, & Honor Your Parents

It was the middle of the month. Barry had met with more than half of the board members and had exactly half of the month left. He liked to stay ahead of the curve; rushing was never fun.

Today Barry was meeting with a renowned pastor to discuss the church's innovative programs to help people with problems, be it relationships, financial, parenting, marriage, or addictions. Christian leaders with help from the secular world had developed many crossover programs using the Bible and modern techniques and ideas.

Based on the alarming statistics presented at the board meeting, Barry couldn't help but wonder if these programs were really working.

"Pastor George, could you describe your recovery programs to me?" Barry asked, after he was seated in Pastor George's office.

"Yes, we are extremely proud of what we have accomplished. We have a robust full-blown weekly program of outreach, teachings, and events using Friday nights and our small group network. The program has been so successful that it has been shared with thousands of other churches and we have trained over twenty-five thousand pastors and their key people. These DVDs highlight some amazing testimonies of our success," said Pastor George as he handed Barry a small package.

Barry took the small box and put it under his chair. "You attended the board meeting, and as I remember, you did wonderfully in that game we played together," he commented. "You understand there are lots of ways to 'skin a cat' as evidenced by the number of successful programs your church has created to attract and retain members. You also know the assignment is to find out why we are losing market share."

"Of course, and I'll do whatever I can to support the Chairman and CEO and will willingly honor their request," replied Pastor George. "What specifically do I need to do?"

Barry explained, "I came to not only meet you and remind you of that request, but to also give further instructions. They want you to interview a family that participated in your recovery programs and find out why they left the program and the church. Specifically, the Anderson family."

Pastor George was making notes, so Barry continued: "In setting up our appointment with your assistant, Hilda, she happened to mention the Andersons. Apparently, she and Julie Anderson were the best of friends. They went on missionary trips and worked on many projects together. Fred Anderson, as I understand, was on the church council, and their two children, Toby and Melinda, were bright lights in the youth program."

"That was true several years ago," Pastor George commented, "but unfortunately they divorced and left the church. Julie lives with her mother somewhere here in town, and I think Fred got remarried. I'm not sure about Toby and Melinda, and none of the family is associated with our church."

Barry asked Pastor George, "That's perfect then, isn't it? Your job is to interview the Andersons, both Julie and Fred, and find out the issues of why they left the church to see if there is anything the church could have done to help them more."

Two days later, Pastor George parked his car in one of the visitor's parking spaces at the entrance of a large apartment complex. It was well maintained with plenty of trees, fountains, and flowers.

He looked up unit seventy-eight as Hilda had directed and pushed the intercom button. An older woman's cheerful voice welcomed him, and she pushed the gate buzzer and he entered the grounds.

This was a nice apartment complex, but nothing like the place the Andersons used to live at in their affluent gated community. Their old house entrance was more impressive than the apartment's well-kept grounds.

He recalled the many fundraisers held at the Anderson's house and at their country club. Black tie, BBQs, golf sign ups, and even a car auction of classic hot rods. Fred was a car collector, and his efforts brought in a lot of money for the church. Julie had been a leader in all the women's events. Both were warm and gracious hosts.

Six years ago, the Andersons came to Pastor George for counseling. Their daughter Melinda was going through a tough time. She had experimented with drugs and sex and was suffering the consequences. Fred wanted to take a hard line of discipline, but Julie wanted to support Melinda with counseling and understanding. Things simply got worse as Melinda, who did not have strong direction from anyone, used the conflict to continue her rebellion.

The counseling sessions were intense. Julie and Fred each used their Biblical backgrounds to support their own positions. Julie was a product of the women's movement, and Fred, although a product of Woodstock and a Cal Berkeley education, was now a conservative businessman with definite philosophies of how to lead a family. Pastor George was the designated referee, though his advice was usually in Julie's favor.

Pastor George focused on getting a line of communication going between everyone, and he recommended that Julie attend women's programs, Fred participate in the men's Bible study groups, and Melinda go to youth camp. Oddly, however, the more they were exposed to the church's Biblical/secular programs and solutions, the greater the conflicts.

When Melinda ran away to San Francisco and moved in with a pimp, Fred and Julie blamed each other. "We should have been more understanding and loving," Julie kept saying, and Fred would reply with, "No, we should have been tougher."

The end result, after numerous counseling sessions and pleas to keep the marriage commitment under God, was that Fred and Julie divorced and eventually both left the church. This was the first time since their divorce that Pastor George had spoken with Julie.

Pastor George made his way up the cement stairs to the apartment. The door was open behind the old style screen door. The TV was turned off as soon as he knocked. Julie's mother came to the door and warmly greeted Pastor George. She attended church on Easter and Christmas because she enjoyed the traditions.

"Come on in, Julie is expecting you," she said.

Seconds later, Julie walked into the living room, looking quite tired and pale. She seemed to have lost much of her self-confidence and vivaciousness. This was not the well-groomed, Nordstrom-clothed hostess that Pastor George was used to. She was wearing something that looked like a housedress Muumuu from K-Mart and quite frankly looked a little dumpy. Nonetheless, she warmly reached out and hugged Pastor George as though reuniting with a long-lost friend.

They both expressed their joy in renewing their relationship, even if it was only for the day. Pastor George quickly explained, "Julie, I'm here for two reasons. First, just to reconnect and find out how you and your kids are doing. Second, if you would be willing, I've been asked to follow up with key people who have left the church in order to find out why they left."

Pulling up a chair at the kitchen table, Julie stated, "Sure. Have a seat. Let's talk." Pastor George pulled out his paper and pencil as Julie moved some books and sat down. "Melinda's life has been destroyed. She attempted suicide twice. She's in a detention facility now. Toby joined the Marines. He said he needed to change his life. I think he's doing fine, but he's in Afghanistan and his life is at risk. Me? I'm not who I was."

"I'm so sorry," Pastor George replied. He had enough experience as a counselor to know that a glib answer would do more harm than good. "And what about you? How are you?"

Julie flicked her hair out of her eyes and answered, "I've been thinking a lot about what happened. How could it happen? I had everything — a devoted loving husband, wonderful children, friends, a great walk with the Lord, and a strong base with my church family. Of course I have my mother, and she's been a great support, but I've lost every-thing."

Before Pastor George could make a comment, Julie showered him with questions, "How could this all happen? Why has the Lord forsaken me? I'm embarrassed to go back to church. Being single, free, and not under the authority and protection of a good man is not that great. Fred has moved on, but I'm stuck. How do I get unstuck? I've had a lot of time to soul search and try to figure what I may have done. Have I disobeyed the Lord? Is it me? I'm so glad you are here. Do you know why this has happened? Can we talk about this together?"

"Sure, let's talk about this further," Pastor George remarked, blinking his eyes several times. Blinking his eyes, he knew, was an internal sign that he not only had no clue as to what was going on but that he was also feeling some personal guilt for her situation. "Hopefully I can help."

Julie poured hot tea into two mugs and took Pastor George to a bench in front of a small pond and fountain in the apartment garden. She had spent many hours here reading her Bible and other books and praying about what had happened. She had earnestly looked for answers, and now that Pastor George was here, she was anxious to go deeper.

As soon as she sat down, she began, "Pastor George, in my journal I tried to recreate what happened. Fred was a devoted husband. He was faithful, hardworking, and took his family responsibilities very seriously. He tried to provide everything to make me happy. Why then did I feel emptiness and that I wasn't getting enough from him?"

"Hmm," Pastor George replied as he made a few notes. "Tell me more."

She continued, "As you know, I believe in the empowerment of women. We should be able to have it all without having to submit to a male-dominated culture. I believed that men kept women 'barefoot, preg-nant, and in the kitchen,' and in the workplace, they used the glass ceiling to keep women in their place.

"Well, I met Fred in the early 70's at Berkley. We both were anti-war, anti-establishment, anti-authority, grass-smoking hippies who were supported by our authoritarian, doting parents. Question authority! Light up, drop out! We were for any cause that would upset the 'man' — civil rights, peace, drugs, women's rights, socialism, children's rights, and even animal rights. Fred supported me, and we had an equal rela-tionship. When we got married, things began to change. He was about to be drafted, so he volunteered and joined the Marines. He spent two years in combat and came back a changed man. Then he got a job with a high tech company in Silicon Valley, became a capitalist and, believe it or not, started voting republican."

"Things changed, but was it Fred or just the fact that you were getting older and carrying more responsibilities?" asked Pastor George.

Julie acknowledged, "I thought it was Fred, mostly. As we worked hard to live the American dream, I have to admit I became a bit more conservative, but I always proudly maintained my sisterhood in the feminine movement. No man was going to tell me what to do, not even Fred.

"Fred and I coexisted at home. He made the money, and I ran the house and the kids. I also ran our social and spiritual calendar. As you know, I started going to your church and eventually brought in Fred and the kids. I really liked the church. Also, the church supported my feminist stands and seemed to be a partner in freeing women and children from male dominated. I liked that. To keep up with the culture, the church-like society seemed to take an anti-authority, pro-women position and used the Bible to support it."

"Pardon me?" Pastor George stammered, blinking repeatedly. "What do you mean the church supported your feminist perspective? We as a church have always been accused of being male dominated."

Julie opened her journal to a page that she had highlighted and said, "Listen to what I wrote several years ago: 'Though the leadership of most churches is male dominate, it seems that the church, like the rest of society, has accepted the politically correct message. Now it is preached and integrated into all church programs.'"

"Those are pretty tough words," Pastor George objected. "I mean, I don't think many churches, apart from those who went so far as to preach from a gender-neutral Bible, would agree with what you've just said."

Taking a sip of her warm tea, Julie nodded, "I know, but once I wrote it down, things seemed to click in my mind. Remember the marriage vows, of how men are supposed to 'love, honor, and protect' and women are to 'love, honor, and obey'? Well, they don't say 'obey' anymore, do they? It's been totally removed."

"Okay, I'll grant you that," Pastor George replied, "but I don't think I get where you are going."

Flipping to another page, Julie read, "The biggest change was to minimize the Bible authority and hierarchy concept where God is the ultimate authority figure, followed by leaders on earth, which includes the authority of the husband. Does the church preach the fear of the Lord? No. Instead, it's all about grace. Is being obedient to God stressed? No. Are the husband or wife's Biblical roles and responsibilities clearly defined? No."

Looking up, she continued talking, "Let me tell you what this did to me on a personal level. Because of all the support I was getting from my women friends, the media, and then the church, I found myself becoming disobedient to Fred. I started questioning his decisions, his manhood, his authority to be the leader of the house, and his authority in raising our children. I became a disrespectful house critic. I did not want the responsibility of making decisions, just the opportunity to criticize. I started nitpicking everything about Fred."

"Let me clarify a bit," Pastor George said, feeling frustrated. "Are you blaming me, and the church in general, for your divorce and your family situation?"

Julie shifted around on the bench, then replied, "Yes and no. The church, small groups, and Christian counseling all supported my position. Everyone agreed it was the responsibility of the husband to come home and take care of the wife's emotional needs, to be a warm supporter of the children, to help with the dishes, to coach soccer, and to never miss a school event because family is more important than any job. Basically, he was supposed to do everything right, and if not, I had the right to blame him for being a 'typical male.' Now, I recognize that I was the one who did this to Fred, so it's also my responsibility."

"Would Fred ask you about this, about your attitudes and actions toward him?" Pastor George questioned.

With a soft laugh, Julie responded, "He did until he learned that it always led to a fight. I wanted him to do everything right, but I was confused in my role. Our arguments consisted of his solutions and my criticisms. We were supposed to be a team, but he was the player and I was the critic. I was a demanding, unhappy woman rather than a wife who loved, honored, and obeyed her husband."

"And all this came to a head in your disagreement on what to do with Melinda, didn't it?" surmised Pastor George with more of a statement than a question. He was beginning to understand at least a part of Julie's logic.

Smiling in agreement, Julie stated, "Exactly! I did not want Melinda to be restricted by old-fashioned, male-dominated thinking. Fred would get upset with her outfits, but I said all the girls were wearing the same thing. He would be concerned about her boyfriends, but I would say Melinda could make her own decisions. He would want her home by a certain hour, but I said that curfews were just another restriction on her freedom. When she would get into trouble, Fred wanted to discipline her, but I would argue that she needed more understanding and communication. Fred and I were no team at all."

"What does this mean to you now, as you are looking back at it with twenty-twenty vision?" asked Pastor George.

Finishing off the last of her cold tea, Julie leaned back and stated, "Now, I see how wrong I was. I needed to submit myself to God and to my husband. I wasn't being abused, and neither was Melinda. I was simply disobedient to God and to my leader and protector, Fred. Sadly, I encouraged Melinda to do the same."

"I can see how our counseling sessions didn't really address those issues," Pastor George acknowledged.

Turning to face Pastor George, Julie's face had an inquiring look to it. She raised her eyebrows as she explained, "Pastor George, I think the church should support honoring God and men who have accepted the awesome challenge and responsibility of leading a family."

Pastor George blinked.

After a pause to let the implication — that the church was *not* doing this correctly — sink in, she continued, "The church has become feminine, and real men are leaving. Women feel something is wrong but don't understand what it is. I understand now; we've been taught and encouraged to be the critic instead of being part of the team. By not preaching and supporting the Biblical hierarchy, the church is encouraging disobedience to God."

"I have a hard time believing that I'm encouraging disobedience to God!" exclaimed Pastor George. Then, trying to regain his composure, he asked, "Are you saying that your situation is the result of disobedience, for which you are responsible, but disobedience that the church is promoting and teaching?"

Firmly, Julie closed her journal and replied, "Yes, I'm saying that. I'm responsible for my actions, but the church did little to stop me from driving my marriage right off the cliff. In taking away the respect and fear of the authority of God and men and by replacing it with the license to disobey, I see the church as partly responsible for the high divorce rates, lack of discipline to avoid evil, disharmony, disrespect by children, and all kinds of societal problems today."

"Well, I'm going to have to spend some time thinking about what you've said today," Pastor George said calmly, but on the inside he marveled at how many things Julie said matched the concerns, questions, statements, and statistics that the Chairman and CEO put on the table in the boardroom.

Julie added, "When people used to ask who the most important people were in my life, I used to reply glibly, 'God, Oprah, Gloria Steinem, Gandhi, and others.' What a joke that was. Now, and if I ever get married again, I will proudly and boldly say, 'God and my husband.'

That should be what all wives say, for every husband and wife is a team, and God is the only true coach."

"I respect your humility," Pastor George said as he stood to go. "I really do. And what you've said, I promise to get back to you with my thoughts."

They hugged goodbye and Julie headed back to her apartment. Pastor George glanced at his watch. He had an appointment on the other side of town in exactly forty-five minutes. He would be meeting Fred, Julie's ex-husband.

As he drove, Pastor George admitted to himself that his conversation with Julie was troublesome. She challenged much of what he stood for and had developed over the last fifteen years. After leaving seminary, his interest in the psychological side of people led him to combine the best of the Bible with the best practices in counseling and psychology to really help people with their problems. He felt confident his programs were effective, and everyone in his circle of like-minded leaders praised his work.

Now Julie was questioning it. And the boardroom experience, just two weeks earlier, had him reconsidering his approach to the counseling he did, the church's impact, and his overall vision for Christianity.

"They think I'm wrong, but I'm really helping people ... aren't I?" he asked aloud as he drove. "How could she be right?"

He agreed with her logic on many points, but he just couldn't swallow the idea that he was driving people to disobedience.

Pastor George drove up to the corporate rental apartment parking lot. Executive Rentals provided executives on long-term assignments a place to stay for a week or two. It was also a refuge for professionals in transition ... mainly men who were forced to vacate their homes. Fred moved in as soon as Julie asked him to leave. He continued making payments on the house and all other bills while living in a dreary four hundred square-foot apartment that reminded him of his dorm room in college. He had his clothes, personal items, laptop, and the Zenith seventeen inch TV from the guest room. That was five years ago. He could not afford to move. His credit was destroyed by tax liens, garnishments, and the bankruptcy. He had refinanced a number of times before the split to pay for counseling, legal fees for the separation and divorce, and Melinda's criminal cases.

His good friend and boss had been very sympathetic, but eventually Fred resigned because he knew he wasn't carrying his weight at the office. The emotional and financial trauma he was going through was just too overwhelming. His guilt caused him to develop a negative, isolated attitude. He was not the self-confident, successful man that he once was. He was doing sporadic consulting to get by, but the cost to provide for Julia's living expenses and Melinda's counseling and legal fees was burdensome. He never missed any payments, even if it meant borrowing money from his relatives, which he hated to do.

Pastor George dreaded this meeting. He and Fred had butted heads during counseling, and though he had sided most often with Julie, he didn't feel that Fred was much of a listener.

Fred's stomach was also in knots. He took a few deep breaths. Though it had been quite a few years since he and Julie had gone through counseling, he still remembered the feeling of being ganged up on by Julie and Pastor George. Fred was always portrayed as the impatient, solution-oriented bull in the China shop that did not listen to anyone. Pastor George called Fred insensitive and unwilling to express his feelings, and when Fred finally spoke up passionately, Pastor George and Julie admonished him for being too blunt and going too far with the "truth."

The fill-in-the-blank workbooks supported by sophomoric DVDs on dialogue and communication were forced upon Fred. It reminded him of the mindless diversity and sexual harassment training that considered all white men guilty as charged. The exercises seemed to be designed to reinforce that men were guilty by their unwillingness to cooperate with nonsensical, politically correct brain washing.

While Julie had all kinds of support from her women's Bible study, Pastor George, seminar leaders, sermons, and the media, Fred felt that he had no one on his side. Intuitively, he knew he was the leader who had responsibility for his family. But everyone tried to get him to join a collaborative group partnership of equal dialogue and compromise with his wife and children. At home, he was not in charge. He would often tell Julie that he felt like a visitor who paid the bills and who was there to support the family. He was one of four votes.

At work, he was a well-respected executive responsible for a major division of one hundred people and fifty million in budget, but when he lived with Julie and the kids, he had little if any authority. He worked for the family and had to prove daily that he was worthy of that role.

Fred, sitting on the balcony of his third-floor apartment, saw George pull up and start walking toward the entranceway. "Hey, George," Fred yelled. "Come on up. It's number 317."

Pastor George waved back as he walked through the front doors toward the stairs. He didn't want to wait for the elevator. Fred was waiting for him with the door open.

"You're right on time," Fred said as he greeted George in the hallway. They walked into Fred's small apartment and made their way to the balcony. George was tempted to ask about Kathy, but he didn't really want to. He remembered hearing that Fred was seeing Kathy before the divorce between Fred and Julie was finalized and didn't want to go there. Instead, George explained the reasons for his visit.

Fred responded, "I'd be happy to discuss the situation. Most of the pain has subsided, except for the visits to see Melinda in the Arizona women's facility. It is heartbreaking to see my little sweetheart in orange overalls behind a metal screen. I expected to see her at Cal cheering for the Bears, not behind bars. On a better note, I'm proud of Toby, and he's doing well in the Marines. I even hear that Julie is doing better."

"Yes, I actually spoke with her earlier today," said George as he moved on to the main topic. "The board wanted me to interview both parties, with hopes that I could gather helpful information from both of you."

Handing George a Coke, Fred stated, "Well, I really can't ask what her answer was, so I'll just give you mine. I left the church because I thought nobody was speaking up for men. Your counseling just made it worse and undermined any authority I had as a husband and a father. I checked with the Bible, and I believe I'm right."

"I must admit that I knew you would be ready," countered George as he balanced his Coke on the railing so he could write in his notebook. "Is there a specific verse that you have in mind that supports your view?"

Fred immediately responded, "Yes, it's Ephesians 5:33, which says, *'Nevertheless let each individual among you also love his own wife even as himself; and let the wife see to it that she respect her husband.'* They preached this just the other day at the church I attend now."

"Interesting," George replied, trying to stay focused on the problem at hand. "And what does that verse mean to you?"

"The Bible gives us a blueprint of the hierarchy of authority. In this verse, it says clearly that I am to love my wife and my wife is to respect me. Now, I admit that I failed to stay faithful to Julie, but she drove me away, and so did you. Now, what's done is done. I can't go back and fix it. It's too late, but I can say that I've taken responsibility for my actions, and I'm paying the price for my disobedience to God and my adulterous relationship.

"Have you taken responsibility for your actions? And if you have, then why are you still preaching that it's okay for wives to dishonor and disrespect their husbands?"

"I must object!" said George forcefully. "What do you mean that I'm encouraging women to dishonor and disrespect their husbands?" He didn't want to say it, but Fred's comments were strikingly similar to those of Julie!

Fred replied, "I went through your counseling, remember? And I went through your teachings. I know what is said and what isn't said. I've also taken the time to do a little research. I found that the couples you've married, they still have over a fifty percent divorce rate, which is the same as the non-church world."

"I've noticed that sad statistic as well," noted George as he sat forward in his chair. "But I see it as their choice. I can't make them stay married, can I?"

Shaking his head, Fred acknowledged, "No, you can't be the marriage policeman, but if the church culture produces the same results as the world, then I have to question — on the statistics alone — the validity of what you are teaching. Is the church teaching the whole truth or just a portion of the truth?"

"Go on," George said, blinking a few times as he tried to make his notes legible.

Fred explained, "Jesus is my boss and He has delegated His authority to us on earth. Men are to love, even lay down their lives, and women are to help and honor. We all need a leader, someone we respect, honor, and follow. I learned that in the Marines and in business. We just cannot let anarchy run rampant. Of course there are always a few bad apples in positions of authority, but that is no reason to drop the whole system. Get rid of the bad apples. If you don't support that standard, then who will?"

"Our counseling has received great reviews, and it's being used all over the world," interjected George. "It is helping people, and we have many stories to prove it."

Fred stated, "I'm not saying that you stop your counseling programs, but I am saying that you need to add in a strong dose of God's authority, obedience, and order. And no, I'm certainly not pushing for a manipulative, controlling church; we've all seen or experienced those. Instead, we as the church ought to follow an example — God's example, which brings harmony and life rather than argument and divorce. Wouldn't that simply be a reflection of our integrity and our obedience toward a magnificent, wise God?"

Fred added one other point: "I never felt you cared about me, my feelings, my struggles, and my relationship with Jesus Christ. What about love? We never talked about love for God and each other. It was all about Julie and your counseling program. You never showed your heart to me or listened to my feelings. I'm a tough guy, but I have feelings and a desire to do the right things. You never helped Julie and me develop a way we could live together under God. Instead, it was all about dialogue and feelings, not our honor, duty, and commitments.

"In general terms, what does it mean to respect our wives? Do you think I was disrespectful to Julie? Do you think I was a bad husband under God? I think she would admit I was a good husband. What are we men doing wrong that women feel justified in disrespecting us and separating us from our families. Women initiate most of the divorces over 'irreconcilable differences' these days. You and Julie asked me to change. How? I did not ask Julie to change, just love and honor me. What does all this mean?"

"I think I'm following your logic," George responded.

With a look of humility across his face, Fred stated, "If I had been obedient to God, I would have not given up my leadership responsibility at home, I wouldn't have started to see Kathy during the counseling, and Julie and I might still be together. I must add that if Julie had treated me with honor and respect, I would not have sought love elsewhere. And I'll also add that if Melinda had obeyed her parents, she would have not ended up in jail. For that matter, if people were obedient, they would not kill babies, fornicate, drink alcohol to excess, divorce, take drugs, do crimes, and more. It all starts with love, then obedience to God and toward those whom He has given authority."

"Hindsight is always twenty-twenty," quipped George. "But you can't go back and try to relive the past."

Fred replied, "You are right about that, though I do wish I could go back and redo things. I hate what has happened in my life because of my own disobedience, and though I've been forgiven, I must add that only a fool would repeat his folly."

"What do you mean by that?" asked George, feeling that another lambasting was coming.

Clearing his thoughts, Fred let it out. "George, have you been obedient to God in teaching His hierarchy of authority to all of your members? Or are you more interested in developing programs and getting kudos from your buddies?"

The words hit George right between the eyes. He expected Fred's bluntness, but the words were piercing.

Somehow, the meeting ended.

He felt like he was in a stupor as he stumbled back to his car. "Doing these two appointments back-to-back was insane," he mumbled to himself. "I'd like to slap that Barry fellow. Who does he think he is, sending me out on this thankless fact-finding mission?"

But back in his car, George composed himself.

Before the throbbing wore off and before he started the car, he jotted down a few questions to consider later:

Yes or No:

- Have I missed a major component of the Bible?

- Is it my intention to help people live more effective lives under God by teaching the Bible or to look good to my colleagues?

- Was I operating under love or taking positions?

- Is the church encouraging disobedience by not preaching the reality of God's order because people might be offended?

- If so, are we helping people sin?

The questions seemed horrible to consider, but there had to be answers, good answers!

9

A Powerful Role for Women in Christianity

This would be Barry's last face-to-face interview. The rest of the interviews had been and would be over the phone. He didn't mind phone interviews, but meeting in person definitely added an element to the communication.

Pastor Joan was speaking in town and had agreed to meet Barry at the restaurant in a luxury hotel near the Los Angeles International Airport.

Barry had worked with major consulting firms and small youth groups, and he knew that across the board, women were multi-faceted. Some of them played the sexy victim who wanted a rescuer, others tried the tough approach, some were on a feminist crusade, and a few walked the middle ground and knew how to balance the soft feminine side with the need to compete in a male-dominated culture.

"It's not easy running the gauntlet," Barry murmured to himself. Pastor Joan was a first-generation American. Her father, an Air Force pilot in Brazil, had married an American missionary, and Joan had moved to the US when she was nine years old. Before meeting any CEO, Barry would study the company, industry, and trends, and he had studied Joan and her ministry as well.

Like many female Christian leaders, Pastor Joan was ordained but did not have her own church. She had left her original church in Miami and launched out in her own ministry. She had written several books and would regularly give thousands of her books to churches that would in turn give them out to entire neighborhoods across the country.

Her primary focus, however, was on her own TV show that aired in English in the US and Portuguese in Brazil. She was bi-lingual and effortlessly moved from one audience to the next. The people loved her passion and her exuberance, and the fact that she was tall, dark-skinned, and pretty helped as well. Her gift, she stated on her website, was to positively communicate scripture to women and men, challenging all people to fulfill their roles under God.

She appeared on the shows of other pastors and spoke as an invited guest at churches, Bible studies, and seminars. She was in the area and was heading back to Florida.

Barry noticed her as she exited the elevator. She approached his table and asked, "Barry?"

"Great to see you again," Barry exclaimed, shaking her hand without tipping his chair over. "You are not alone?"

"No," she said, "this is my daughter, Isabel. She's traveling with me and is heading back to college tonight. I thought she would enjoy our conversation together, if that's okay with you."

"Of course," Barry smiled, shaking Isabel's hand and pulling up an extra chair. "That'll be good. I'm always looking for an extra perspective."

After giving them time to order, they settled down to talk. "I must confess," Joan started with a laugh. "The game you had us play in the boardroom a few weeks back, where we all were forced to consider our intention, the mechanism, and our results? Well, I played that game with several people in my audience last week, and it was a riot!"

"Yeah," Isabel added, "but I don't know if seeing people rolling across the floor is the best thing for a Christian TV show."

Barry replied, "I'm glad the game was entertaining, but I would probably have to agree with Isabel about doing it behind closed doors. But pushing the boundaries is necessary for people to change their thinking, so if you want to, feel free to keep doing the game."

"I'll keep that in mind," said Joan, bringing the conversation to focus. "What is it that the Chairman and CEO want me to do specifically?"

Barry placed his notebook in front of him and explained, "You heard the assignment about finding out why Christianity is losing market share. With that as the backdrop, we want to get your perspective on the role and future of women in the Kingdom. In the world, you would expect there to be arguments, fighting, disrespect, and sexually motivated decisions, but not in the church. Sadly, there isn't a very big difference between the church and the world in many respects."

Pastor Joan had that "what's new?" look on her face as Barry continued, "There is nothing to gain by you interviewing the Christian leaders and men who have ostracized you from a leadership position in the past. I've heard it said that the men versus women issue is old school. Doing that type of interview would end up with you as the aggressive victim and the male pastors taking a hard-line, scripture-based defensive posture."

"But Barry, I've been fighting this battle all my life, and I'm not backing down now," she aggressively responded. "Are you sure you don't want me to lay it out on the table in front the boardroom? I can do it."

Barry was impressed how composed Isabel remained, watching her mother speak with such emotion. "I know you can fight the battle," he stated, "but we believe now is the time for women to step up as Christian leaders, not just victims or vindictive activists, and to push for true transformation. It is intrinsically linked to the decreasing market share."

"So how can I push for true transformation?" Joan asked.

Sitting forward, Barry explained, "The short answer is that you need to lead by example. I need you to find a woman who is confused and who has made bad decisions that destroyed her life and those around her. I want you to fully understand and present her point of view. Then I want you to respond, not only as a woman, but as a woman of God who responds in a Christ-like way. Your example will be a model for everyone."

"I'm used to men either resisting or giving in, and I can handle that," she said, obviously mulling over Barry's comments, "but you are asking me to lift myself and others beyond the usually petty differences. You are asking me to turn the other cheek, to love, to help transform everyone, and to not agitate for women."

Quite perceptively, Isabel spoke up, "What's sad is that I understand what you are saying. I mean, the fact that we even have to explain that we want to go beyond the norm pretty well defines the norm."

"And that doesn't even address the fact that we all would probably rather stay in the norm," added Joan. "The norm is, after all, our comfort zone."

Barry asked, "Can you achieve this in two weeks?"

"Well, this is undoubtedly a great opportunity to make a major contribution to the Kingdom," as she was warming up to the challenge. She responded. "I'd do whatever it takes to make that happen. I'll do it for women, for men, for the CEO, and for the Chairman!"

Handing her a note, Barry explained, "I have a lead for you, if it fits your schedule. It's a young lady who desperately needs help transforming her life. Her name is Melinda, and she's doing time in a correction facility in Arizona. One of the other pastors from the boardroom met with her parents. If it doesn't work out, I figure you have plenty of leads back home."

"This is interesting," Joan replied, looking at the note. "I think I'll call the mother first and see what happens from there. Isabel is heading back to school, and I technically have an extra day or two. Perhaps this will work out."

Barry thanked the women for their time and headed to the parking garage where he had parked his car. Joan had to get Isabel packed up for her return trip but was able to put a call into Julie, Melinda's mother, who was already in Arizona for a regular visit. "If you can get to the airport here, I'll pick you up and take care of all the other arrangements," Julie offered.

As if it were planned, Joan was able to rearrange her schedule so she could stop in Arizona, spend time with Julie and Melinda, and then get a flight out the next day. Perfect timing.

Julie was excited to meet Joan. Joan represented a woman of God who was tough, loving, caring, and effectively successful. Joan provided the model: a feminine woman who was also a warrior. Joan could, with humor and incisiveness, say things to women and men to shake up their beliefs and get them to take positive action.

Julie said, a few minutes after meeting Pastor Joan, "I hope you can help Melinda. She's confused and bitter. She's rebelled against everything and destroyed her life."

"I understand that," responded Joan. "I have spent a lot of time with women in prison trying to understand why and how they got there and what to do to help them make better decisions in the future. I've written many letters, mailed countless books, and visited many of them behind bars. They are all confused. That's part of the reason that they are in there in the first place. The confusion starts with their fathers, their boyfriends, and/or their husbands. The feminine movement, the secular culture, and the church's reaction don't provide any answers. They aren't just confused; they are bitter as well."

"Yes, bitter is the right word," remarked Julie. "Maybe Melinda's bitterness is her reaction to the confusion within her. I don't know."

The thirty-minute drive seemed to last just minutes as the two ladies chatted. Julie turned off the main highway, and bumped along the dirt road until they came to the minimum-security facility and its fifteen-foot high razor wire fence. The light gray buildings were the only sign of civilization for miles in either direction.

"There are two hundred women here," Julie explained, pulling into the parking lot. "They can't leave, but I also wonder how they will ever learn to love their families or function in society again. It's a temporary prison term that seems to have life-long repercussions."

"That is so true," Joan responded. "My heart melts for the mothers, daughters, sisters, wives, aunts, and grandmothers serving time. I've met and prayed with many women in prison. Most, in hindsight, will tell you that they have made bad decisions along the way. It's usually a story that includes sex with the wrong man, marrying for the wrong reasons, drugs, crime, running away, an abortion, divorce, etc. The wrong decisions and choices add up over time."

"One decision after another, one choice after another, and slowly they inch their way here," pondered Julie out loud as she looked at the facility.

"Well said," Joan replied.

"Say, that reminds me," stated Julie, "Melinda sent me a note once that included a bunch of short half-quotes from other inmates. It was so true and so real that I kept it in her file. Here it is."

Joan took out the folded piece of paper and opened it up. It read:

- "I'll show my dad ..."
- "I'm leaving home ..."
- "I'm dating the wild boy ..."
- "I'll have sex with whoever I want ..."
- "I can make my own decisions ..."
- "I don't need you ..."
- "It's my body ..."

"It seems that women are rebelling against a male-dominated society," Joan noted, "but ironically, the more they try to fight men, the worse their predicament and the greater their regrets."

"I know, but yet you can't really blame men for the bad choices these ladies, including Melinda, have made," replied Julie, as she stuffed her purse under her seat. "Sometimes I just can't figure out what's going on."

"Uh, why are you jamming your purse under the seat? Is the car safe here?" asked Joan.

Julie explained, "I put everything, all my books and notes, in this cardboard box. They don't do a strip search, but they do inspect everything you bring in."

"I want to also say," Julie went on, "I believe you can tell Melinda things that she will receive from you but won't from me. So, thank you from the bottom of my heart for that."

"My pleasure," replied Joan. "I really mean that. And some day, after you and I write a book together, let's see if we can get other women to do the same."

Julie laughed, not sure if Joan was serious or not.

The guard at the gate checked them in and gave them directions. From there, after the screening and meticulous searching process, they made it to the meeting room where inmates were allowed to meet around tables with approved guests. Melinda was waiting for them as they walked up.

"Hi, Mom, it's good to see you," Melinda said, giving her mother a hug.

"You too, honey," Julie replied. "I brought a new friend with me today, Pastor Joan. I figure you've probably seen her on TV."

Melinda, distrusting of all authority figures, female or not, quietly shook hands with Joan, and they all sat down.

Joan began. "So, Melinda, tell me why you're here."

Melinda's eyes narrowed. "Because I was caught with drugs again and violated my parole," she replied. "You knew that, right?"

"I'm not interested in the legal reason," Joan responded. "I want to know why you believe your life has led you to this facility. What happened to you?"

Melinda looked at Joan. She had been through hours of counseling by the best. She knew the game: display anger about being mistreated and misunderstood, then express deep hurt and emotional rage that forced her to take a different path. Melinda started by recalling her past turmoil with her over-controlling churchy parents who tried to manipulate her into being the "nice little church member and daughter who made them proud."

Then before Joan had a chance to ask another question, Melinda spoke from her heart, "Honestly, I hated it when my parents would argue about me in the kitchen. I heard it all from my bedroom. They wanted me to be this good little girl, and when I would rebel, they would try the latest Biblical, pop psychology technique on me. It was disgusting and totally unreal. Sometimes I just wanted Dad to grab me in his big arms and not let me go out. Or Mom to tell me she loved me and wanted to protect me. I didn't need her to try to be my friend or to rescue me from Dad."

"I'm so sorry," Julie replied, a tear running down her cheek.

"It's okay, nobody can change the past," Melinda stated. She sighed, "Okay, I admit that I was a spoiled brat who needed someone to take charge of me. Looking back, I was not ready to make my own decisions. Imagine being ten years old and driving a car without being able to reach the brakes and without knowing any of the rules. I know I claimed that I was smart enough and all grown up, but you let me drive, and I crashed my life."

Joan just let Melinda talk.

"My dad could tell the boys who picked me up were not right for me, and he was right," Melinda admitted. "They got me drunk, gave me drugs, and got me to do sexual things that were horrible. After that, I could never look my dad in the eyes again. In school, I was pegged as a 'slut' and a 'party girl' who would do anything. I was in the wrong crowd and could not get out. Then we started going to Hollywood, where I met evil men, not just boys. I had to lie to my parents to continue, and it got worse. I felt I was no longer part of the family."

"But you were always part of the family," interjected Julie.

"I knew that at a mental level, but at the emotional level, I did not belong," Melinda explained. "That Christmas I attended church with the family, I saw some of the boys at church I had sex with. I was embarrassed, as well I should have been, and after Christmas dinner I vowed I would never go back home. Looking back, I realize I had isolated and destroyed myself and nobody could help me. The truth is, I was crying out, 'Somebody stop me!'"

Both Joan and Julie cried silently as they listened. They realized this was an extreme but common story of a little girl growing to unprotected womanhood in our society.

Joan asked, "Where are you today in your thinking"?

Melinda replied, "I'm not sure. I know what doesn't work, and that's taking the road of rebellion, bitterness, and bad counsel. I know my results suck. Look where I am for the next two years! I've been reading a lot, including the Bible, but I'm confused about Christianity. If Christ is the answer, then I have not been asking the right questions or something. I am open to change, but can you show me something that works?"

Joan hesitated. She did not want to give a simple solution or cliché. She knew Melinda was sharp and would reject anything that sounded condescending. "The fact is," Joan began, "I'm here on a mission from God. I've been asked to explore the question, 'Why is Christianity losing market share and influence?' And I'm looking for ways we can change and improve, so let me turn your question around to you. Can you give me your honest thoughts about what you really needed when you were growing up? What was it that you really wanted but didn't get?"

They talked and they cried together, and about an hour later, Joan noted, "You've talked a lot about things you missed and what you wish you had. Where does love fit into all of this?"

"Well, I knew mentally that my parents loved me," Melinda replied, "but I would say that I really needed a love that protected and disciplined me."

Joan concluded, "I am impressed, Melinda. In all of your thoughts, questions, and concerns, you have asked some really good questions that will eventually lead you to the right answers, I know it. In addition, you have helped me see even more that it's not at all about men's rights versus women's rights. It's about being real, it's about loving others as

God intended, and it's about submitting ourselves to those who love and want to protect us. Thank you. And do you mind if I share the notes we've written together with the other board members when I meet with them?"

"Fine with me," Melinda replied.

"And let's stay in touch, all three of us, as we walk this journey of life, and especially during the time you are here," Joan concluded.

"I would like that," both Melinda and Julie said in unison.

Their time was up, so after several hugs, Melinda was taken back to her cell and Joan and Julie headed back to the car.

"I'm not sure who got more out of our time today, Melinda or me," Joan remarked. "This has been good, really good."

10

Real Life
Transformations

After burning a lot of midnight oil to keep the board members on track, interview them, push-start a few, gather the results of their interviews, and then compile the information into a practical, easy-to-use format, Barry was ready to wrap this up.

From experience, he knew that the most difficult part of working on major consulting projects was the act of putting all the pieces together. Every consultant had his or her own perspective and way of doing things, yet all the data had to contribute to the overarching theme, and everyone had to support that theme.

Barry had already started to draft reports and hold follow-up appointments with each pastor in preparation for the boardroom presentation next week. Time to get ready for the ultimate "come to Jesus" meeting.

To Barry's surprise, when he arrived for his follow-up meeting with Pastor Joe, Joe was waiting downstairs in the church office's lobby. "Good to see you, Barry," he said, putting out his hand. "Come on up. I know we don't have much time, and I have a lot to talk about."

Barry followed Pastor Joe up the stairs, taking them two at a time. So much had happened in the past few weeks. It was hard to believe he had been here just one month ago.

Pastor Joe seemed fresh and alive. "You said you wanted to know what I learned from my meeting with Halden Mack at the Veterans Hospital," Pastor Joe volunteered, even before they sat down. "Well, you got my report, but it's not what I learned that affected me so much as what I felt."

"Tell me more," Barry responded, quickly flipping open his notebook. "Your report had a lot of details that I can use in my presentation, but I am very interested in knowing what happened to you on a personal level."

Diving right in, Pastor Joe explained, "This may sound terrible, but in speaking with Halden and thinking about what we discussed, I came to the realization that I had lost touch with my personal relationship with Jesus Christ and His people. Consider Halden. He is so committed to Jesus, he was willing to die for his buddies, yet he considers the church to be completely irrelevant. That combination, that reality, struck me to my core."

"How so?" Barry asked. "If I remember correctly, his words to you were pretty harsh."

Nodding, Pastor Joe stated, "I want you to hear what I'm about to admit. I've only told my wife thus far, but here it is: I realize now that I considered the church to be my main obsession ... and that I used Jesus and the people to build my church. The people were an audience for me to wow. I wanted them to do things to enhance my ego and reputation, and they did it because I was so persuasive. The simplicity of Halden's comments forced me rethink my priorities."

"Go on," Barry encouraged, only partially taking notes. "This is a big revelation that could have a far-reaching impact."

94

Pastor Joe took a deep breath, then continued, "We've lost touch with the young soldiers, and in fact, with the young people in general. We've been focused on the wrong things. We assumed that young people needed to be entertained and treated like the frivolous twenty year-olds in beer commercials. That's not true at all! Only Jesus and soldiers will die for us. These soldiers volunteer to be separated from their families and are willing to be subjected to long periods of hardship and even death. That's serious stuff!"

"I agree, but what can you do?" Barry asked.

Pastor Joe's excitement bubbled over as he explained, "As brothers in Christ, and with great humility, we need to partner with the young soldiers to find out what we can do together to bring us all closer to Jesus. What can we learn from them? What happens when they come back? I'm not just talking about platitudes about honoring our soldiers on Flag Day, but about transforming what we do and with young people serving the Kingdom of God. We need to listen and come up with something more powerful than uniform day or hospital visits or cookie bakes. We need to get back to the basics. We need to bring the soldiers' passion for Jesus into the church."

Barry took a few more notes as the meeting wrapped up. He couldn't help but be impressed with the diminishing ego and positioning from Pastor Joe. "That's a good beginning," Barry said to himself.

As he stood to go, Pastor Joe added one last comment. "In one of our initial email exchanges, you said something that I didn't fully understand until now. You said, 'When you are emotionally touched by another to the point of considering change, change will happen.' I want you to know that I completely agree with you, and I welcome that change."

"Very good," Barry exclaimed, then he headed out the door and down the stairs. Thirty minutes later, he was back in his own office, getting ready for three phone appointments that same afternoon. There were other calls scheduled throughout the week.

The first call would be with Bishop Mike, the man who had burned several bridges on his journey toward his fourth church appointment. Barry didn't like the vibes he got from the man.

The phone rang. It was Bishop Mike.

"Hi, Barry," Mike said, sounding friendly and chipper. "I've actually got a golf game in twenty minutes with none other than John Carrington. You remember John?"

Barry replied, "Of course I do. You told me all about him and Helen and how you two had been able to, miraculously it seemed, put a relationship back together."

"Yes, that's right, and you will get a laugh out of this ... do you know what Helen told me the other night when I called?" Mike asked. "Well, I'll tell you. She said I was, quote, 'less self-absorbed and intellectually condescending,' end quote. Can you believe that? And what's even more funny, I actually laughed with her about it!"

Barry took notes as he discussed these unexpected changes. "That says a lot, not only that she felt safe enough to say it, but that you laughed with her. That means what she said is no longer true."

"I agree," Mike responded. "John and I have talked a lot about understanding businesspeople and their responsibilities. I admit, I felt threatened by most businessmen, but one day John told me, 'You run a business, too. You have employees and customers, just like the typical CEO.' I can relate to the responsibility they carry, and the fact that these business owners play a financial part in so many people's lives is really amazing. What an honor, and what a responsibility!"

Barry asked out loud, "Is this the same Bishop Mike that I spoke to just a few short weeks ago?"

"Now that is funny," Mike replied. "I have even attended a few board meetings here locally. There were great discussions about how to serve customers and act responsibly in the community, lift up people, create abundance, make enough money to provide for everyone now and in the future, and more. I realize now how childish I must have sounded as I ranted against businesses. And on top of that, I've met business owners who take better care of their people than I do. Talk about embarrassing!"

Smiling to himself, Barry acknowledged, "What's most important, I'm learning, is that you've grown and changed. It doesn't matter what you used to do, it matters what you do now. So, good job."

"Thanks," Mike said, slightly changing the subject. "I've got to go in just a minute, but I wanted to add one more thing. The great heroes of the Bible, like David, Solomon, Abraham, and others, produced great wealth. God likes success and in fact wants all of us to reach our given potential. John challenged me to think bigger than ten percent. Instead of preaching against prosperity, I intend to be the catalyst for the other ninety percent of the resources to grow. I want to plant seeds and encourage growth to create massive abundance."

"Now that's an amazing realization," Barry exclaimed. "What will that mean for you, practically, as the Bishop?"

"For starters, rather than preaching sermons on giving ten percent, I'm going to preach on multiplying the ninety percent," explained Mike. "Instead of merely encouraging the wealthy to give and share a portion of their wealth, why not challenge them to maximize their talents to create great abundance for all in the Kingdom? Isn't poverty a lack of wealth? Christianity can produce increase in all areas, not just money. I just need to encourage the masters, servants, and families to focus on sowing and reaping a bigger crop. Expanding the pie is better than guilt-ridden sermons on sharing a cupcake."

Barry replied, "Wow, Mike, you amaze me. I really mean that."

"Well, I used to preach the parable of the rich young man as a justification to poverty and the rich giving to the poor, but serving two masters was the real issue for the young ruler, not the fact that the guy had money," Mike admitted. "God did not banish the wealthy men in the Bible. In fact, God spoke of blessing David, Abraham, Solomon, and others with increase and abundance, and yet these guys were already wealthy. Also the story of the talents, the owner rewarded those who risked and got a return on their talents, and he punished the servant who buried his talent. God praises those who are good and faithful servants."

Taking notes, Barry asked, "So, Mike, what does that mean on a practical level for other pastors? I mean, in the boardroom when I present my findings, what would you suggest that I say?"

"All that we've discussed is important," explained Mike, "but I think I would explain how we as pastors need to unleash all the power and resources for the Kingdom. We in the churches only influence ten percent, but if we negatively impact the ninety percent like I have been, then we are harming the Kingdom. Why do we need to give to the poor? Because they have no money, of course, but we should be finding out why they are poor. How can we lift people out of poverty rather than simply support their poverty? And how can we do so while following Biblical principles?"

Barry nodded, "I like your logic. I take it that you have already studied this?"

"For the past week I have been discussing with John a certain Christian venture capital fund that works to jumpstart economies. I'm changing my sermons to focus on increase in all areas of everyone's lives. I realize we've been sending mixed messages to our business leaders. Money is not evil; it's the love of money that is wrong. Poverty is not godly; it is actually against what God wants for us. Flourish, multiply, prosper, be diligent, work, but don't cheat. Anyone who praises poverty is causing poverty. How could we be such intellectual snobs? How can we unleash the power for the Kingdom, Jesus, and the people? I believe 'Christian innovation' is the term that best describes it. Some might see that as an oxymoron, but it's not."

The bishop was already late for his appointment, Barry knew that, so he quickly finished up the conversation and let Mike go. After they hung up, Barry flipped back through his notes with Mike. "Quite a change in him," Barry commented to himself. "I certainly didn't expect to see that, but if he can change and if he can speak into the congregations under his control, then that's great progress."

After a short break, it was time to focus on the next interview. It would be with the archbishop. He dialed the number and was put right through. "How are you?" Barry asked politely. "Thank you for taking the time to talk today."

"My pleasure, Barry," the archbishop responded, then added, "I must admit, when you first called several weeks ago, I did all I could to excuse myself from the required research. I don't think I wanted to stop and address any real issues."

Letting out a slow breath to ease any tension, Barry stated, "I remember that. It sounds like you've made some great progress then?"

"Oh, you haven't heard? Then I guess my report hasn't yet arrived in the mail," the archbishop explained. "I mailed it because I included some newspaper clippings that you will enjoy reading."

Barry liked the sound of this. "Tell me more," he responded.

"Well," the archbishop paused to clear his throat, "I was truly devastated by my meeting with Jack and truly inspired by the kids he works with. They poured love and acceptance on me, the last guy who deserved it. I had forgotten what really matters, like love, compassion, and integrity in my quest to lead and protect the church. It had become all about the organization and my own ego, and like most people who experience a major tragedy like divorce, death, or automobile accident, it jolted me to reconsider what matters most."

Barry asked, "What did you do, then? I mean, I've heard it takes over a mile for a cruise ship to stop, so it's not like you can just stop things that have been put in motion."

"You are right, it does take time for some things to stop," the archbishop agreed, "but internal change can be instant. What I heard and experienced that day with Jack, I took personally. I came back and reviewed everything I did and started to make changes. I turned over to the authorities the names and files of pedophile priests whom I had been protecting. I stood up to my superiors and their lawyers and fought for doing the right things. I wasn't sure I would be welcome anymore or if I would keep my job, but the laypeople I meet are loving it and embracing my honesty."

Circling the word "integrity" on his notes, Barry was about to ask a question when the archbishop jumped in.

"Do you remember how I needed to travel with security and how people would yell at me when they saw me in public?" he asked. "In the short few weeks that I've had to unravel the web of confusion and lies and cover up, I've noticed a drastic change. I mean, people actually smile at me now. Sure, some still rant and rave, but the change is already starting to happen. I never would have believed it!"

Barry prodded, "Tell me more about the changes that took place inside of you."

"That's easy enough," the archbishop replied. "I feel like my resentment has been replaced with love and forgiveness. I no longer blindly trust and protect priests who have done something wrong. I expect the truth and repentance. Nothing less. Also, and more importantly, I feel like I have a whole new personal relationship with Jesus. My prayers are not just the clichés and platitude-type prayers any more. Now, it's about real love and openness and self-disclosure. Instead of pondering, searching, and complicating matters, I've gone out and gotten dirty. Last week I ladled out stew at lunch to the children at Jack's orphanage, and this afternoon I'm going over there to play basketball with some of the boys who simply need a friend."

Wiping away a tear, Barry commented, "I can see why the people you meet on the streets are acting different ... because you are not the man you were."

"Oh, how true that is," the archbishop stated. "How true that is. I feel so light, as if a burden has been taken off my shoulders. The more I walk in compassion and love, the lighter I feel. I think burdens fall away when we live lives of humility and service. That's what I'm coming to understand."

Barry needed to bring the meeting to a close. He had one more call to make. "Thank you for your time," he said. "I look forward to reading all that you've sent me. When it gets here, I'll follow up."

The once-hard board members were changing, one at a time. It was great to see, and very encouraging. The last call was with Pastor George. "Too bad we can't do a conference call with Julie and Fred as well," Barry thought to himself.

The bright spot with Julie and Fred turned out to be their daughter, Melinda. Pastor Joan had kept Barry up to date with almost daily emails about her ongoing conversations with Melinda and Julie. Real change was taking place, and it was great to see.

The phone rang. It was Pastor George. After a few short pleasantries, Barry dove right in, "Tell me about your meetings with Julie and Fred. Did you find answers that we can report in the upcoming board meeting?"

"To tell you the truth," began George, "I think if Julie and Fred had hung in there longer, they would have discovered the real issues about their relationship and would have been able to work it out. This applies to their daughter, Melinda, as well."

Barry replied, "Yes, it seemed that way from what you wrote in the report. What else did you find?"

"I think it was a lack of faith in Jesus and the process," explained George. "I have lots of couples who benefited from our approach. Julie gave up and Fred continued to resist till the end. What I learned encouraged me to try harder and to not give up on myself. Yes, maybe we need a chapter on commitment in our training module and maybe we should recreate the wedding ceremony as a small group exercise and get more accountability partners, but I don't think we need to go back to a rigid, male-dominated abusive system. Where's the heart in that? Jesus was not abusive. I still think men have to learn to be open and share their authority. We're not extremist Muslims, are we?"

Barry asked for clarification, "So, you are saying that you don't believe that the hierarchy outlined in the Bible is relevant for today's society and issues?"

"Yes, of course I do, but we can't be rigid," replied George. "Take some divisive issue. Shouldn't we love people and accept them, regardless of what they do? Wouldn't Jesus do that and not be rigid in his reaction? The same with marriage. We shouldn't use the Bible to imprison the weak and abused. We need to give equal justice to the weak and down-trodden don't we? Women should have a choice about what they do with their bodies, and that means their sexual freedom and their right to choose. We should not be rigid or dogmatic to the point that we have no compassion. If people, because they are human, make the wrong choices, shouldn't we be there for them and not be critical?"

Barry was biting his tongue. It seemed that George had not changed in the slightest, but perhaps he would amaze the whole boardroom. "I will let you present your findings and recommendations at the board meeting," Barry stated.

"Yes, I would like that," stated George. "I need to tell it like it is, and we as a church have a lot of experience in these issues. I see men, women, and children as equals, and communication and dialogue can solve everything. In many respects, authority is old fashioned. You need to be open to everything. And if you hear of any negative responses to the trainings we use, the reason is that the individuals are resisting."

Barry knew from experience that once the members of a board saw the truth of a situation and started to change, the momentum would become positive peer pressure. As a result, they would be very harsh on those who refused to change when directly confronted with powerful truths.

11

Back to the Boardroom

Barry was back in the reception room, waiting in a leather chair outside the boardroom. Just forty days ago he had been called in to help with this very big project. Would it have worldwide implications?

Most people don't talk about what God does to those who are disobedient. Adam and Eve were kicked out of the Garden, and man was forced to toil and woman to endure painful childbirth. The flood destroyed all of mankind except for Noah and his family. Sodom and Gomorrah were destroyed. And in the final book of the Bible, Jesus — the loving, compassionate savior — will ride down on a white horse with a drawn sword to fight the devil and clear the world of non-believers.

Hell, though it was not created for mankind, is where those who reject God will spend eternity. Barry asked himself, "Do these spiritual leaders remember this as they preach the right hand (love) only and not the left hand (toughness), except when it comes to church attendance and tithing? If God is all-powerful, as they preach, do they fully realize what that can mean?"

He looked down the hall for the Chairman's assistant. Everything was quiet, except for the murmur of voices and the sound of chairs squeaking from behind the boardroom doors.

This meeting was not just a reprimanding sales meeting where bonuses were reduced, harsh words uttered by the boss, and even possible terminations. No, this was really a life or death meeting. There was no Plan B. It was all or nothing.

Barry was energized by the upcoming challenge.

Thumbing through the big Bible from the coffee table, Barry glanced through the verses in red. It reminded him of a conversation he had had with a group of Christians many years ago. They kept coming back to the position that Jesus was all about peace, harmony, and feeling good about themselves.

"Read the verses in red," Barry had suggested. "Jesus was love embodied, and that love commanded respect. Jesus had holy anger against the works of Pharisees and the works of the devil. Jesus was brutally real with the Pharisees and wasn't afraid of turning tables. He wasn't a doormat, and He was no pushover. It was His kindness that attracted the masses to Him, and His truth that set them free. He didn't ask how they were feeling, yet He was gentle, kind, and compassionate. He was the total package of love."

Angrily, someone had asked Barry, "Are you saying that reading and discussing the Bible, raising money for missionaries, collecting gifts for orphans, making food bags, the adopt an angel program, and things like that are of no value?"

Barry had responded, "No, of course not. They are certainly important. You are to take care of the poor, the weak, the sick, the widows, and the orphans; but that is not all you are to do. Jesus did not spend much time on these activities. Salvation is a gift, but it was bought with an extreme price. God gave so much, yet it is so easy to take it for granted."

"So what are you proposing?" someone else had demanded.

"What if Christians went upstream before people drifted downstream into support ministries?" Barry had offered. "Of course you should help those in need, as the Bible commands, but out of love for others shouldn't Christians be leading and bringing about change before they are called in to help clean up the pieces of a broken life?"

"That is a huge task," the leader of the small group had stated.

Barry had agreed, but countered, "God is bigger than all that. Consider the heroes of the Bible. David would have received no credit for crushing a midget. No credit for Moses leading a two-week tour for sightseers interested in the Middle East. No credit for Noah building a boat in a bottle. No credit for Joshua conquering a small village of lepers. And no credit for the disciples putting on a book-signing tour. Not good enough! God wants you to accomplish big things, things that go way beyond your ten percent tithe, being nice, intellectual self-discovery, and debating prowess. You cannot be distracted by the good, because God expects you to be great."

A few weeks later, Barry had met again with the group, but they were different! They had expanded beyond Bible study classes and support groups and had become interested in upstream causes like training boys and girls, discipling young men, helping single mothers get on solid ground, and much more. The individuals in that group went on, in their own ways, to positively impact countless lives.

Barry glanced up. The Chairman's assistant was coming his way. "Just a few more minutes and we'll call you in," she said.

"Okay, thank you," Barry replied.

The assistant slipped back into the side office door. Barry would be going in shortly. This was going to be a tough meeting for many of those in the room.

Speaking of tough, Barry remembered one of the board members telling about his father's perspective on tough love. The board member's father had owned a pool hall, and when two guys would start a fight, he would yell out, "If you want to fight, let's go outside. And when you're done, I'm going to beat the crap out of the winner." That stopped a lot of fights.

This dad was tough, yet he was loving and generous at the same time. The board member had explained how he both loved and feared his dad. "By nature I wanted to be disobedient," the member had said, "but I knew the rules and the persona of my dad, and I acted accordingly. His favorite quote as I sat at the counter in the pool hall was, 'Don't be a bum like that guy. He doesn't take care of his family.' I remember that to this day."

As their interview progressed, the board member had made a pretty tough statement. He said, "God and Jesus really exemplify tough love. Their actions are always a mixture of strength and kindness, wisdom and discipline. We, on the other hand, always seem to complicate and confuse issues to avoid accountability and retain our own agendas." Barry had agreed with him.

Barry knew the boardroom was going to be energized. He could almost feel the excitement seeping under the doors. From experience, he knew that the combination of new perspectives connecting with truth and other people always revitalized and challenged individuals and groups to step up. He also knew that pain was part of the breakthrough and that some people in the room would not be part of the team. Most board members are motivated to be part of a team that is growing, changing, and moving to win, but not everyone makes the cut.

Barry had a personal bond with most of the leaders, having gained their trust and respect by pushing for the truth and relentlessly asking them to stretch their perspective and reconnect with basic principles. Probably ninety-five percent of them wanted to do the right things, but many of them succumbed to pressures, their own egos, and their comfort zones.

The final meetings with board members, when Barry presented his findings and suggestions for growth, always seemed to have a strong rallying cry that caused the players to support the team ... or leave. Being chosen was the ultimate for a player. Being thrown off the island, not making the team, getting fired, or being put on the bench was a strong motivator for super achievers!

Why then are the Christians losing market share? Statistics flooded Barry's mind. It was then that the massive boardroom doors started to open.

12

The Ultimate Come-to-Jesus Meeting

All the board members greeted Barry with hugs and high fives. They were like a little league team ready for the finals. The excitement was mixed with fear and trepidation, but it's what makes life worth living!

It was time.

Barry made his way to the front, and as everyone sat, the Chairman stood up. He looked serious and yet smiled at Barry. "Are you ready for our next agenda item?"

Heads nodded around the table.

The Chairman added, "Barry, as we discussed, I want you to be the catalyst for the discussion. My Son and I will jump in only if necessary."

Again, heads nodded. Hopefully, heads wouldn't roll.

Barry picked up the PowerPoint controller and stood near the white screen. "Good morning, everyone," he began. "I'm going to slightly dim the lights because I also have a written report that you'll be receiving in just a minute. In addition to my content, all of you will be presenting your preliminary findings and assessment as to why Christianity is losing market share. Please keep you presentations to less than five minutes. Your combined analytics and reports that you gave me are included in the folder you will receive."

Several assistants began handing out black binders that contained almost one hundred pages of data, graphs, quotes, and more.

"What the Chairman and CEO are looking for is a major transformation that will reverse the situation," Barry continued. "We may not solve all the issues, but truthful awareness is the first step toward change."

All the board members now had a packet in front of them, and most were flipping through it.

Barry went on, "Before we start, I want to explain that typically people push against change. They resist it. That's natural. If I encourage, challenge, or even push you toward change, please recognize that we are all on the same team. With that said, I want to give you a quick template that I use to stimulate discussion among powerful people in a boardroom."

The room dimmed a little and the first image appeared on the screen. It read: WHATR5.

"This template will help us think in new ways so we can combine the intangible with the tangible," Barry explained. "The **W** is for Winning. Are you winning? You might be winning individually, but the team Christianity is losing. Look at the overall metrics. At thirty-two percent and declining, you are not winning as a team.

"**H** is for Harmony. Are you in harmony? You can't be in alignment with the world and with the Father and Son at the same time. Remember, you are *in* the world but not *of* the world. And this lack of harmony doesn't even address the people you deal with on a regular basis.

"**A** is for Attitude. What is your attitude? Are you negative and blaming or positive and aggressive to get this done? What is your attitude, and what are you sharing and spreading? Based on what the average person says about you, do you think you have the best of attitudes?

"**T** is for Truth. Are you telling the truth? This has two applications: one is the truth of the Word, and the second is the truth of your situation. This is key, for the truth will set you free. The question of your truthfulness usually comes up during a crisis or when the powers that be call you on your attitude, behavior, and results. Have you been seeking the truth?

"**R** is for Right Things. Are you doing the right things? Right doctrine, right message, right information, right people in the right places, right goals, right strategy, right use of resources, right values, right ethics, and right focus. If you aren't getting the right results, it's questionable if you are doing the right things."

Barry paused. Nobody was reading the binder. They were all taking notes.

"The WHATR elements are the intangible questions you need to explore before you get to the specifics. Often I can tell just by listening in a boardroom what the answers are to the WHATR questions. We need to get clear on the intangibles first. Then we will move to specifics and the tangibles.

"Next, the 5 stands for the objectives that you will set out to accomplish in the next ninety days. We need everyone in the boardroom to focus on results, and we take what needs to be done and what can be done in a typical year and condense it down to just ninety days. Perhaps in your world forty days seems like the norm. It doesn't matter whether we use ninety or forty, the key is urgency to meet the objectives."

Barry went to the next image on the screen. It read:

> ## #1 Objective: Rehire or Recommitment.

"In the corporate world, I usually ask the board to rehire the CEO in two weeks. That's their biggest job. If they agree to rehire the CEO, then he rehires his key people. In this case, however, the Chairman and CEO do not need to be rehired, so our focus is going to be on you, the executive team. In short, within two weeks, everybody here will either be on board or will be gone."

Barry paused, not only for dramatic effect, but to let the truth of this sink in. This was not a game or a job with no requirement for high standards and great results.

"Think of it this way," Barry explained. "Every season with a sports team you have to try out in order to make the team. You are chosen, and in this case, you will be rehired based on your performance, potential, and commitment to the new strategy. I've seen some board members who choose to self-select off the team because they could not join in full harmony and commitment for the new path. It's one hundred percent in or out, no fence walkers!"

The volume of chair squeaking increased. Barry knew it would.

Barry clicked the PowerPoint button again. On the screen it read:

> ## #2 Objective: Target four other goals.

"Time for taking concerted action toward four goals that you agree to target," Barry continued. "Often it's a new program, new clients, ways to raise capital, compliance, or earnings that a board chooses to deal with during those ninety days. For you in this boardroom, it could be a new strategy, a campaign to change minds, gathering more data, a recommitment to your purpose, or something else. The meetings that are held ninety days later usually boast amazing results, with ninety percent of the goals being met. Those teams are on fire! Of course, that also means that those boards have ten percent fewer people. Not all are chosen to go on."

The lights went up and Barry walked to the corner of the conference table. He looked around the room, trying to make eye contact with everyone. "Are you ready to begin?"

"Yes!" said several in unison. Most nodded their heads, but a few were staring back at Barry, showing no emotion.

"You are the ones who will receive all the attention," Barry went on, "because you are the operating people on earth where the thirty-two percent market share applies. You will present your findings. I don't want to pressure you, except for you to realize that your findings and your new attitudes are going to be key regarding your position in the Kingdom. It's like the parable of the talents. Some of you will get more responsibility based on your ability to handle it. Basically, this meeting is your opportunity to demonstrate your potential to turn things around and make it happen for the Kingdom."

All the fidgeting in the room could have generated electricity if it could have been harnessed.

"With that said," Barry said, stepping away from the table, "I would like to call Pastor Joe up to be the first presenter. Please tell us what you found and what you're going to do now."

Pastor Joe pushed back his chair and made his way quickly to the front of the room. Despite the fact that he was the first, he looked quite confident and serious. He pulled out his notes and began, "My brothers and sisters in Christ, I come to you today to admit my pride and arrogance. I was serving myself and my church, not God. I lost touch with the people and the Lord. I made it a metrics-driven business. Not the metrics we discussed, but the metrics of seats, tithing, church attendance, baptism, budgets, publications, conferences, programs, DVDs, and books. Granted, we helped a lot of people, but we missed our main calling, and that is to serve Christ and to serve people."

Joe's bold step of humility would have an impact on every presenter after him — Barry knew that much. Barry was also impressed by the fact that Joe was so open and humble. He really didn't have to do so, but it was fresh and invigorating.

"As you can see in my report," he was saying, "I visited Halden, an injured soldier who had just returned from Iraq, at the local VA. I quit visiting hospitals years ago because I wanted to use my talents in other areas, but Halden opened my eyes. His real relationship with Jesus, the reality of death out on the front lines, and the honesty of his pursuit after God — not to mention his disdain for my church — really shook me up. You all know that my church is one of the largest in the world, but I had lost touch with people. Most importantly, I had lost sight of my personal relationship with Jesus. I am proud of our accomplishments, but I am more proud of my new relationship with the Lord. I am also grateful to be Halden's friend."

He stopped for a second, his voice quivering. He wiped away a tear and continued, "We need to go back to basics. That should be one of our corporate goals. I'm working with Halden to help the young people coming back from combat and to help them get closer to Jesus. I'm not completely sure where this will lead, but I know I'm going in the right direction. No more interviews on Larry King or Oprah or big PR campaigns. Instead, I'm going to connect with the young soldiers and listen, learn, and serve the Lord together."

The room was silent. They were used to Pastor Joe's big vision and business metrics, intimidating as they usually were. They admired and respected his achievements, but this was the first time they saw his heart for the Lord.

Without giving anyone time to clap, Barry stated, "Next I would like to call Bishop Mike to talk about his interviews with a businessman who left his church."

Bishop Mike slowly approached the front of the room. His brashness seemed to have been replaced with timidity. "I thought I had everything under control," he began, quietly yet clearly. "But I have come to realize that I was using the pulpit for my own ego and political views. I also realized I had bigoted ideas about business people. I guess it came from my liberal college education and political ties — I don't know — but I picked verses from the Bible to reinforce my opinions and intolerances."

He glanced over at the Chairman and CEO, seated at the end of the table, and then back to everyone else in the room. "I'm sorry. I've already asked forgiveness for that, but I knew how to manipulate most congregations with my knowledge, charm, and powerful sermons. It was the businesspeople who would stand up to me, and most were kind enough not to call me on my stuff. They usually went along with me unless I openly insulted them, like I did with John Carrington, a strong supporter in one of the churches that I led. He was, and still is, a very successful businessman. He tried to work with me until I used my position to ostracize him and criticize him for not giving more of his money to the church and for questioning my authority.

"Upon Barry's insistence, which was the directive to all of us, I set up a meeting with John. We both talked, we both listened, and it was an eye opener for me. I don't have to agree with everything John says or does, but I have discovered how I can work with him, and other businessmen, to unleash that power for the Kingdom. Unless we reach out to the businesspeople in our churches, we are limited to ten percent of the resources for the Kingdom. John and others have access to the ninety percent, so what can we do to work together to create abundance that really helps the poor? I want to learn more. I want to open myself up and be more inclusive, not just for businessmen to help my church but also for me to help businesspeople really help the Kingdom. I have chosen to change so that I can accomplish this goal."

Again, the room was quiet. "Archbishop," Barry spoke up. "You are next. Please come forward."

Everyone looked at the archbishop as he glided to the front in his robe. He always felt a little out of place with this group, and being the only board member wearing a robe didn't help at all. Many of the members had mixed feelings about him. There were denominational conflicts, and some would argue that the Catholic Church was not even Christian.

Like a democrat senator speaking at a tea party town hall meeting, he cautiously began, "I was shocked at the last meeting at the Chairman and CEO's assessment of our accomplishments on earth. I know we've all been struggling, but had no idea things were so dismal. I know I have been prideful and in denial. I've blamed the secular world, governments, the culture, media, lawyers, and even other competing Christian denominations for our own slide in market share and impact. So when Barry asked me to reach out to a former priest, I was resistant. Couldn't I just send an intern?"

Several members laughed. They had thought the same thing, no doubt.

"What could I learn from Jack, a priest who showed his lack of commitment to the church by walking away several years ago? Not much, I figured, but boy was I wrong. My report in the folder does not reveal the whole story. Jack opened up my eyes. I realized I needed to go back to the basics. I had lost my purpose and relationship with Jesus in favor of a relationship with men and their institutions."

As the archbishop looked around the room, Barry sensed that others had just elected the archbishop to be part of the team. It was a special, unifying feeling.

"We need to stop sin at the source," the archbishop stated emphatically. "Jack and Barry and others call it going upstream before people begin going downstream. Honestly, we've become so downstream oriented, with all our support groups, causes, and fundraising, that we have lost our ability to catch people and connect them to the source, Jesus Christ.

"We were always proud of our Catholic schools, particularly in the inner city. We were able to graduate fine young students at a lower cost and with greater skills than the public schools. Why? Because we taught the discipline of Jesus Christ and the Word, but we've lost that edge. In fact, we allowed a virus — the virus of priest pedophiles — to infect our church. I take personal responsibility for letting that happen in my area and will do all I can to stop it, but I will add, as you all very well know, that this virus is not only in the Catholic Church. We all need to step up and do what's right, to reestablish our own personal relationship with Jesus Christ and to work upstream as well as downstream. Upstream is harder, but that's where we need to focus our efforts, and the Bible tells us how."

The archbishop held up his hand, as if to ask a question, and then he looked at the Chairman and CEO and stated, "When I looked into the eyes of the young boys at Jack's orphanage, I painfully remembered my dereliction of duty to honor my Lord, my vows, and my heart. I vow to follow your commandments no matter what the pressures are."

Both the Chairman and the CEO nodded.

"Pastor George is next," Barry said, breaking the spell of silence and awe that was in the room. "We will take a short break after Pastor George finishes. I will say that I am feeling some powerful emotions and transformations taking place here today. You are on your way!"

Pastor George stacked his notes at the front of the table. He began by telling of his meetings with Julie and Fred, and though all of it was in the report, he shared their honest responses about how they felt the lack of emphasis on obedience to authority and the church's counseling destroyed their relationship and family.

"They both told me that they should have kept their promise to live their marriage under God," George explained. "It was their disobedience that scuttled their marriage, not my, as they called it, 'effort to seek truth other than God's Word.' We have helped many couples through our highly effective counseling programs."

Then Pastor George did the famous Yes/But routine that politicians often use. "Yes, we all are sinners and could be more obedient. Yes, Fred and Julie should have been more obedient. And yes, we could have emphasized the hierarchy and Word of God more ... but that doesn't mean we should disregard all the research, writings, and thinking that supports family counseling, does it? Why do we have a mind if we are not allowed to use it?"

The room was silent. Barry could feel the camaraderie and team effort seeping out of the room. It was like Pastor George was a lawyer, arguing his case, interpreting the Bible like the Constitution, and using it to support his own argument or sermon of the day.

"There is too much sex, self-centeredness, and an unwillingness to listen to the church," George stated. "We are offering wonderful programs that combine the best of today's techniques and God's teachings. If Julie and Fred had tried harder, they could have done it. I see the culture to blame for their breakup. What's more, if they had only trained Melinda better and encouraged her to participate in our church youth programs, she wouldn't be in jail today. As a family, they strayed away from the church, despite all the good work we did as the body of Christ to keep them on the path.

"I conclude that we need to intensify our efforts, improve curriculum, get more accountability partners, and be tougher in our approach. I feel for Julie, Fred, and Melinda, but we cannot change our programs because of a few isolated incidents of failure. I commit to working even harder."

All this time, Barry had been watching the Chairman, and when George finished, the Chairman sat forward and rubbed his chin. He wasn't looking very pleased.

Finally, the Chairman spoke. "George, you've got it wrong. The Word reigns supreme. We've given you simple instructions. It's not rocket science. Do you know why I sent my Son to the world? He went and suffered death on the cross and was raised from the dead, thus conquering death, to allow those who repent for their sin and rebellion to come back into a loving relationship with me again, which has been lost since the Garden of Eden. Do you need a Bible Study 101 refresher course?"

He paused briefly, but nobody was going to say anything.

"Consider it like a vow, promise, or covenant you have accepted, not a set of rules and nuanced interpretations," the Chairman went on. "The Pharisees used the rules for their own interpretation and benefit. It is your liberal theology that is weakening the foundations of Christianity, and that is one of the reasons why you are losing market share."

The Chairman hammered George with powerful rhetorical questions that caused the rest of the board members to look down. Collectively, they were hiding from the penetrating, personal questions thrown down like lightning bolts.

Finally, the Chairman asked, "What about you, George ... did you really love Fred, Julie, and Melinda? I mean, really? Did you serve them in my name or yourself in the name of your programs?

"Lastly, George — and others in this room — you are not attorneys arguing your case. You are followers, and you need to start acting like followers. Before our next meeting, I expect you all to ponder these questions and have better answers from your heart. And George?"

George raised his head, which had gone through a dozen shades of red, and said haltingly, "Yes?"

"I expect you to listen, learn, and follow."

The CEO stood at that point and spoke up for the first time, "Let's take a ten minute break, and then Barry will continue."

The room was deathly quiet as the board members filed out the door to the restrooms or the coffee pot. Precisely ten minutes later, they returned, and for the rest of the afternoon the presentations continued. Some went well, some not so well, but nobody bottomed out as badly as Pastor George.

The last presentation would be by Pastor Joan. Barry had planned this in advance, hoping that Joan would ensure that they would go out on a high note. Barry introduced Pastor Joan briefly and let her begin.

"Barry has asked me to present as a follower of Christ, not just as a woman," Joan began. "So I'm not going to talk about the women's issues in our society and in Christianity. I'm not going to talk about the current condition of women as ordained pastors. And I'm not going to present myself as an activist for women's rights. We could discuss and debate so many things, but that's not the point. To do so would bring disunity. Instead, I'm going to discuss our common goal: to be Christ-like."

Joan pulled out a piece of paper and explained, "I made a short list of qualities that apply to us all. Qualities such as: protecting, supporting, providing, serving, and caring. And qualities that should not apply to any of us, such as: abusing, exploiting, criticizing, gossiping, or nagging. God made us, male or female, and His character is to shine through us so that we can live lives, raise children, and work in such a way that please Him and brings Him glory. I believe we have lost market share because we have failed at this most basic level."

A lot of heads were nodding in agreement.

"Who are the key players in a family?" Joan asked, not expecting an answer. "It's the man and the woman. Both are vitally important. And as the husband is the head of the household, and he leads with love, honor, respect, and protection, we women should be the helpmates God intended and provide care, support, and strength. Why do we fight and quarrel when we are on the same team!"

Several of the men quietly clapped in approval. Some may have expected a feminist rant from Pastor Joan, but she was taking the higher road.

"My report is on a young lady named Melinda," Joan was saying. "You heard about her divorced parents, Fred and Julie, and how they are trying to put their lives back together. Well, Melinda is serving time in Arizona as we speak. Can the Melindas of the world benefit from the love and direction of our Lord Jesus Christ? I know so, or I wouldn't be in this business. Young people and those young in the Word are seeking answers to important life questions. Have we been turning them off by glibly providing our solutions without any real understanding of their needs and where they are? Do we really listen? I think we are causing people to do the opposite of what we stand for."

Joan went into the details of Melinda's story and the heart-felt needs that she and Melinda had outlined. She flashed the list up on the screen. It read:

- She needed wisdom, not confusion.

- She needed direction, not preaching.

- She needed the ability to understand, confront, and defeat evil.

- She needed support as a child.

- She needed to know the Word.

- She needed standards of love and discipline, not excuses.

- She needed to be part of something that was bigger than her own wants and her parents' wants.

- She needed a personal relationship with God.

- She needed men who would love and protect her, starting with her father and eventually a husband.

- She needed women to teach her how to be a great woman.

- She needed to serve others and not be so self-centered.

- She needed love most of all.

The room was silent. It was evident to all that the problems were bigger than men versus women or Church doctrine versus secular solutions. The solution required God's help.

"Melinda is really just a typical person," Joan explained. "It makes no difference if we are male or female. It is obvious that we have left God out of our lives. We try to go it alone. We offer our own opinions, and in so doing, we adopt the world's values and systems; but the world is lost and dying. We are so quick to get off on tangents about rights and responsibilities instead of staying focused on the real goal, which I believe is all about knowing God's love and bringing His love to the world through every work, profession, and relationship we can. Sure, women can lead, and so can men. Women can inspire and teach, and so can men. Who cares! Let's function properly and fully in our roles as men and women, and let's teach that to those who otherwise would be lost and confused. I believe most will choose Christ."

She stacked her notes, looked at the Chairman and CEO, and said, "Here's my vow: I vow to promote the Word of God at the highest level of good. I will drop my own earthly ego and commit myself to love God with my heart, mind, soul, and strength, and love others as I love myself. I will use my influence and leadership to motivate women to serve God and to serve others, whether it's men, women, or children. I will use my influence to encourage men to lead with love, understanding, and support under God. I will encourage men and women to use all their talents in His service. I believe in diversity, but I will strive for unity as a higher Kingdom principle and value."

Everyone was inspired. A loving, powerful woman was leading the cause for Christ. It was time for all the board members to raise their vision to a higher level.

It was Barry's turn to give a final assessment. He stood and looked at everyone. "Thank you all for your presentations today, and for the research and time that went into it. No doubt you have learned a lot. I certainly have. It is evident, however, that we are not all on the same page. Remember, I explained that not everyone will be part of the team going forward, whether it's because you choose to leave or because the others choose not to include you."

Barry held up a piece of paper that was not included in everyone's folder. "This final assessment lists several generalities that are affecting you as a group. First, there is a glaring disconnect or lack of harmony between you and the leadership. This is evident by the fact that you have failed to achieve the objectives of the Chairman and CEO.

"Second, you have taken a path comfortable with your modern group beliefs. You have a different interpretation of the Bible than God intended. This has gotten so many Christians, churches, and ministries off track that they have no idea where they are.

"Third, you have lost touch with the fear of God. Have you lost understanding of your subordinate relationship with God? It is His grace, His life, and His redemption that we are talking about. It isn't anything that you have done.

"Fourth, as the Chairman has said, your liberal theology has weakened the very foundations of Christianity. You have to get back to the basics of God's love and His heart for people, and build on that foundation. It is strong and it will last, and it will get you the desired results."

It was a short list, but it got the point across.

The CEO stood up and spoke. "Barry is right. There are many more details and examples that could be added to the list, but you understand what he is saying. Let me tell you directly, though — not from anyone else's interpretation — what this means. It means you have been focusing on small issues and even irrelevant issues and have forgotten the big issues. If you don't turn this around, who will? Come back next month with better responses. Some of you are on track, but you all need to get moving faster."

The CEO looked at Barry to continue. "In the next forty days, you are to take the lessons learned today and commit to major changes," Barry explained. "Remember the game we played about intention, mechanism, and results? This is your chance to bring about change in your heart, commitment to the Chairman and CEO, and action that gets the proper results."

The CEO sat down, then added, "Barry will continue to gather research on his own. I want you all to go deeper, do more, and learn more. I want you transformed by our next meeting in forty days. You simply have to figure it out."

The mood was one of serious silence. Obviously, there was much yet to do.

13

Uncovering Satan's Strategies to Destroy Mankind

Three weeks had gone by since the big board meeting, and though most of the members seemed on track, they were not moving fast enough with a unified focused purpose. Barry felt they had moved from forty percent to almost seventy percent effectiveness, but that was not good enough. They simply had to hit at least ninety percent effectiveness before their final meeting.

From experience, Barry knew that the team needed a major push, but he didn't know what to do to get the needed push.

Just then, he received a text message from the Chairman's assistant. The Chairman wanted to meet briefly.

Barry returned to the corporate office. When he walked into the waiting area, the Chairman was sitting in one of the leather chairs and the CEO was in another. "Take a seat," the CEO said with a smile.

The Chairman began, "We've been talking, as you know, and we want to make a proposal that will shock many of the board members. It's on purpose, but we believe it will have the desired effect. We want you to interview their competition."

"That's right," the CEO interjected. "You will interview Satan, and you will capture in clear print what his motives and techniques are. The board members need to hear it. Don't worry, we'll be with you every step of the way."

Barry responded as logically as possible, though his stomach was instantly in knots. "What you've proposed makes perfect sense. Satan is shrewd and undermines you at every turn, but will an interview give Satan attention that he does not deserve?"

"That's what some people will think," stated the Chairman. "But this once, giving him some attention will have the desired effect on the board members. They need to know that he is real and what he is up to. Also, addressing the competition will fire up the team and motivate them to win, not just stew in their guilt, fear, and weaknesses."

The CEO noted, "Satan went underground many years ago because he wanted to be covert and have a major, invisible influence. He has a base in Los Angeles, but he travels all over the world and sets up his operation wherever he can stir up people to follow him. The meeting is already on the books."

"Bring back a full report," said the Chairman.

Barry stood to leave. The assistant called him over. "You'll have to memorize this, as I can't write this down," she explained. "At 2:00 a.m. tomorrow morning, meet a black Mercedes at 54th and Crenshaw."

At 1:45 a.m., Barry was standing on the corner. It was a cold night, but his mind was racing. The sirens going off from two different directions and homeless men sauntering by didn't even faze him. Barry was trying to mentally prepare himself for the most unexpected interview of his lifetime.

Suddenly, a black, glossy Mercedes pulled up and screeched to a stop in front of Barry. The darkened tinted windows fit the car. When the rear door opened, Barry got in quickly and shut the door. Two large, expensively dressed men were in the front seat. They did not speak. They didn't even look back.

They drove the back streets until they reached a warehouse district, lined with old factories. At a dilapidated auto transmission garage that had long ago been closed and boarded up, the car pulled to a stop. Barry was escorted down several steps into an empty cement car pit to a door that opened to an elevator. The elevator slowly descended two or three stories, and Barry found himself in a dark basement.

Barry could barely see a shadowy figure seated in a chair at the end of a large table. One of the silent escorts shoved Barry into a cold, hard folding chair. A deep voice said, "Barry, welcome to my boardroom."

Voices in the shadows laughed at their leader's joke.

"The Chairman must be concerned," the voice said. "He's losing here on earth. I don't think he realized how I could influence people to turn from him."

Then, turning his full attention to Barry, he said, "So you want to know what the competition is doing. I'd be happy to tell you, because I cannot be stopped. It's time for me to get some credit and recognition for my successful campaign of revenge. The loss of market share is because his leaders don't understand how to appeal to the market. I give people what they naturally want. Did he show you a bunch of bad metrics?"

"Yes, quite a lot of them," Barry stated, with as clear of a voice as he could muster.

"Ha!" he crowed, "What is funny is that all his bad metrics are my good metrics. One of my key metrics is how many people come to hell versus go to heaven. I'm winning that one! I'm the equal opportunity fun god on earth, and people love it."

Minions around the room seemed to love it as well, as they let out a whoop of laughter and cheering.

"So, you want to know how I captured the market? What my strategy is? Well, I can't wait to tell you. No one has asked before because they don't even think I exist. That's part of my plan, of course. It's like a secret chess game with the invisible man. I win most of the time. I don't need to talk about how I got here, but I'll just say that when I left heaven, I came to rule the earth. I think the Chairman wanted to test man to see if mankind would follow him and resist me. The fact that I win most of the time must be driving him crazy!"

More laughing and cackling.

"My first win, with Eve in the Garden of Eden, was the just the beginning," he continued. "Good old Adam quickly followed suit, and their disobedience spiraled the whole world out of control. You might say I started sin. I was very busy then and lost track of time, but it seemed like just a blink of the eye and along came the great flood. Almost everything he created was washed away! Do you know what that taught me?"

Not at all surprised, Barry played along, "No, I can't really imagine."

"It taught me patience," he said with a sneer. "I knew there would never be another flood, so I could take my time. We concentrated our efforts on Noah's family, and it didn't take long at all until we were up to our old tricks, right boys!?"

The roar of delight and rage was deafening.

Finally, when the noise died down, the voice went on. "I'll tell you what I do, as my plan is perfect. I simply tempt and encourage people to do what they want to do. This gives them immediate pleasure and more power and authority to run their own lives. I help them to rebel and demand fairness and justice for themselves and others. What's wrong with that? Nothing, and that's the beauty of my approach. What I do is natural. It doesn't take any discipline to follow me. I just let you go in the natural direction you want to go. I give you encouragement, whether it's immediate physical pleasure, ego respect, or intellectual rationalization. It's a great sales approach, a no brainer for sure. I give them what they want and don't charge anything for it."

Barry spoke up, "But you demand a huge price in the future."

"Oh, right you are!" laughed the voice, "but tell me, who is going to buy into the sacrificial 'follow the narrow way and get your great reward in heaven' approach? Come on, that's lame! I give people what they want, and they want instant gratification. I don't demand any immediate payment, but yes, there is a massive balloon payment at the end, like credit card debt gone wild. It's easy money. It's our little joke. It's hell to pay, literally and eternally, but people are more than willing to strike a deal. In fact, they are lining up to join."

More screeching and laughing. The noisy minions were starting to irritate Barry. "God has a different reward and payment plan," he stated. "And He wants ..."

Cutting Barry off, the voice joked, "Yeah, yeah, we know, you say he gives life. Then why all the rules on how to think, what people can't do, and what people have to do? And the offer of eternal life is pushed way out into the future. According to his leaders, followers can't have sex, money, drugs, or rock and roll. That's unnatural and that's no fun. Totally ridiculous! On top of that, those who don't follow him are automatically mine. I get my own customers and his rejected customers as well. I really have too much business, but who is complaining! I love my work!"

"What's your strategy?" Barry asked before the stupid little urchins could start giggling.

"My first strategy is to give them what they want at no charge," he explained. "I encourage them to buy now and pay some time later. 'You deserve it.' No doubt you've heard that line. Christians want to hold you down, spoil your fun, and tell you what to do. I tell people that they are smart enough to run their own lives and make their own decisions. You don't need silly old rules from the Bible or any authority to govern your life. Free yourself. Open your mind. Do your own thing. Throw off the chains of oppression. That's my strategy.

"Then I help target people who they can demonize or blame. This creates a strong reason for freedom and a cause to fight for. Let's take sex for example. Parents want to spoil the fun and churches are boring. I tell people of all ages, 'It's your body. You have the ultimate choice. Do what you want.' This has spawned the sexual revolution, which swelled my ranks like you would not believe. The Chairman hates sex before marriage for many reasons, and I will admit that it causes a lot of problems ... so I made it a freedom issue, and people went to bat to destroy each other, as well as the institution of marriage."

On a roll, he kept on going. "The freedom of choice has been a great argument for abortion, one of my greatest mindset rationalizations of all time. It's helped free women from male domination, which did wonders to further subvert women, further enslave men to pornography, and further separate man from woman. It's helped push minorities into the limelight, thus destroying many black communities because they were given the right to blame the white society, and with an attitude, they destroy their own. In all of these, who can argue against freedom, choice, and equality? This has created a cycle: I undermine one, that undermines the next, and so on. The further down the chain people go, the less chance they ever have of getting back. It's a riot!"

At his pause, the impish voices cheered with delight.

"What about the truth?" Barry asked, trying to get his words in before the chorus got too loud. "The Bible says the *'truth will set you free.'* Doesn't that slow you down?"

Now the imps were yelling at Barry.

"They don't like it when you quote from the Bible ... none of us do, but I understand your question," he said. "That's my other approach. I slightly distract people from the truth. I get them off track just a little bit, and in time, they will inevitably miss their mark. Remember, I'm a patient guy! I've distracted pastors to focus on small stuff and move away from the powerful messages of the Bible. Then I added humanism to their sermons and programs. That's why the Chairman is so angry. His leaders stress what is important to them, and to everyone else. These things are indeed important, but it's not the Chairman's top priority. As a result, the top priority issues get marginalized. I'm telling you, every Sunday morning, we are down here laughing our heads off. We have multiple big screen TVs set up along the wall and we watch hundreds of churches at a time. It's very seldom that we have to change the channel. Most are focusing on items of no real importance to the Chairman's Kingdom. And the beautiful thing is, they don't even know I'm involved."

More laughing from the dark recesses of the room. Barry wanted desperately to get some fresh air.

"Why do you hide down here?" Barry asked. "Wouldn't you lead a better revolt if you came out of hiding?"

"I am purposely covert, and that is not hiding," he said with a sneer. "I flat out hate people. They disgust me. Every one of them! Is that a weakness of mine? I don't think so. It's my perspective, and that reality won't cause any shockwaves on the surface. People expect it, I guess. Maybe it's printed into their DNA or something, so me staying off the radar, that's part of my plan. I want people to think that they are living life based on their own decisions and rational thinking. I just plant a few seeds, and they take it from there. If I were to go topside, people would be forced to choose between me and the Chairman, and I don't think that would be very fun."

Flipping to another page in his notebook, Barry was about to ask another question when a dark voice spoke up, "Master, tell him about major coup 317."

"Ah, yes. Good point!" he said. "The separation of church and state has been one of my crowning victories in this country. The founding fathers are turning over in their graves on that one. I have successfully taken God out of the schools, ripped right from the belly of the Christian schools themselves. What a joke!"

That part of recent history was not a news flash. "Yes," Barry agreed. "Yale, Harvard, Stanford, USC, and many other state colleges, they were originally schools that trained men for the ministry."

"The emphasis is on *were*, if you please," Satan laughed. "That's a good one, I must say. Thank you for setting that one up. Anyway, I planted the seed about separation of church and state and then I got the government to threaten colleges that funding would be withdrawn. And, presto, it was God or money, and money won. Well, actually, I won, but I'm not publicizing that fact. This secular mindset is now deliciously working its way into the churches."

"You must be proud," Barry stated with his own bit of sarcasm.

"That's funny," he quipped, "and yes I am. You see, by taking God out, it created a vacuum that they fill with elements of my domain, in media, education, and government. They are doing my bidding, but again, I'm not broadcasting that to the world. These young minds are now either anti-God or intellectually open to everything under the sun, which means either way I've won. Brilliant, yet again!"

He held up his hand to stop the inevitable chorus of demented laughter and said, "Want to hear another great one, this time about this country's government?" Maybe he was getting tired of the minions as well.

"Sure," Barry replied, "though your handiwork has been visible there for many years."

"No doubt that's true," he chuckled to himself. "Thanks to me, the government funds schools that keep God out, it funds abortion as a woman's right, it funds welfare that keeps people poor, it funds causes that were not even dreamed of a few years ago, and it funds many other wonderful things. As a direct result, it controls the minds, behaviors, options, and money. It's a government that is increasingly without God. Brilliant, huh?"

Barry asked directly, "So, does political correctness have a number associated with it?"

"That's major coup 589," came the same voice in the darkness.

Barry noted to himself, "He must be the treasurer or the keeper of the minutes. Every board has a brainiac."

"Political correctness started small, but I knew it would spread into all areas of society," Satan said with pride. "I waited patiently, and now, everything you say has to fit into templates of behavior and speech, whether you are on a bus, in school, at the mall, on the radio, or in church. This affects everything people say and do, and that in turn pushes so many buttons at the same time that we can hardly track the resounding results: diversity trumps all, tolerance in the name of anything except Christianity, new laws, rights, and equalities that have destroyed the authority and ability of truly capable leaders, the blame game, perversion in the name of art, and more. It's hard to fathom the destruction that it's caused. Everybody loses! I'm brilliant. I am the king!"

Things were not looking bright. Barry commented, "By giving people what they want, planting intellectual seeds, pitting one against another, rejecting responsibility, offering rebellion and disobedience as good things, all at no cost now, I can see why you are winning. How can they love God and each other when they are so wrapped up in resentment, resistance, and revenge?"

"Let me describe how this works," said the dark voice. "People start with great principles, then I get them focused on creating and enforcing rules. God's principles to help mankind — such as the Great Commandment of love, the Great Commission to spread that love, the Fruit of the Spirit, the Golden Rule, and so on — actually work ... but I work to distort it each and every time. Remember when Jesus said to render to Caesar what is Caesar's? He didn't ask the Romans to tax people to provide for widows. No, he asked the people to take responsibility for the widows and not to force others to pay for the poor. I love it when some politician or leader uses one of God's principles and then proposes a rule to force others to pay or lose a freedom."

Barry questioned, "I don't quite see the connection. I mean, I see how this gets people to focus on the rules, but doesn't that still get the job done?"

More laughing from the darkness.

"Not many people realize that once they become rules-oriented they lose the power because they lose sight of God," said the voice. "My little focus-on-the-rules strategy has destroyed countless marriages and families, divided nations, and led to major wars. Hitler's atrocities were part of his desire to lift up and rule over the German people. In churches, I appeal to the Pharisee mentality where rules are more important than love. Jesus had the greatest problem with the Pharisees, and the Pharisees were the ones who killed him. So I pit the self-righteous against each other, and, voila, another coup for me!"

Holding up his pencil, Barry was beginning to see the situation more clearly. "But if people really analyzed their beliefs and rules and whether they were godly principles or not, the whole world would change, wouldn't it?"

"Very perceptive," mocked the voice. "Of course things would change, but things won't change because people won't change. They are too proud. They love being right and enjoy blindly imposing their rules on others. I am going to keep on winning! Brilliant, isn't it?"

Nodding, Barry stated the obvious, "Yes, it is pretty clever, but God is far stronger than you."

The little imps were quiet, thankfully.

"Yes, God is more powerful than me, but that's not the question," he breathed, seething with anger and defiance. "I rule the earth. His followers are not capable of turning things around, which is why I'm proud to tell you my strategy. And if God comes down and wipes out mankind again, I'll be happy and I'll win again!"

Barry felt a cold hand on his shoulder, and he stood before the chair was yanked out from under him.

"Barry, good luck with this assignment. You're going to need it! The truth is, those board members aren't going to change. You should quit while you are behind."

As Barry was being pushed toward the elevator, he looked back and said, "I've seen transformation already among the members, and I'm confident that the CEO and Chairman are on the right track."

The jeering and hissing only stopped when the elevator doors closed shut. "Phew," Barry said, his face both white and flushed, "I think I need some time to decompress."

When the elevator doors opened, he walked up the cement steps to the black car that was waiting for him.

14

Making Plans with the Father and Son

"Barry, what you have done with these leaders on our board has been amazing," said the Chairman. "Your interview with Satan, which was certainly an exception, will be a good push for the team."

Taking his seat at the side of the conference table, Barry looked up at the Chairman and the CEO who were sitting in two chairs at the end of the table.

"Thank you," Barry stated.

The Chairman continued, "Remember the game that kids used to play in school where one child makes a statement and then tells it to the next person, and on down the line it goes? At the end, the message has no resemblance to what was first stated. Well, that's what has happened to our simple message.

"They don't have to be rocket scientists to understand our message. My Son walked around and spoke the message to people who couldn't read. Fishermen, tax collectors, prostitutes, and common people were the audience. It was the educated Pharisees who overcomplicated our message for their own benefit. Our message was and is for everyone."

The CEO added, "Between people butchering our message and Satan influencing people in the wrong direction, it is little wonder that people have gotten so far off track. We created man in our image, but have given him a free will. Of course we are all powerful and all knowing, but we did not want puppets."

"There's nothing more rewarding," said the Chairman with a heart of love and passion, "than to see our children grow up and do the right things, all while respecting and loving us. We want the best for our children, so you can understand how it breaks our hearts to see them take the wrong path and destroy each other."

Barry could really see, and comprehend, the pain in the situation. The Chairman's eyes watered as he explained, "That's why we called the emergency boardroom meeting those many weeks ago. What we are talking about is a big cause. This is not a good cause or an important cause. No, this is the greatest cause of all time, one that changes the world. We want our children to go upstream and use the wisdom we have given them. We want them to be like a giant dam that keeps everyone upstream. To go with the flow is easy, but it leads straight over the waterfall; and as you know, that leads to hell on earth and eventually eternal hell.

"Anyone can fall downstream. It's natural. And as you heard first hand, Satan knows this reality and influences the unwary with instant pleasures. They have no idea that it will cost them their souls at the end, not to mention a meaningless and oftentimes horrible life on earth, so they succumb and start the downstream ride. Sex, as that was Satan's example, is wonderful and safe, and we designed it that way, but only between a man and woman who are married. Outside of that, it produces nothing but painful consequences. The instant pleasure now turns into broken promises, unwanted pregnancies, abortions, AIDS, depression, the breakup of families, jealousy, anger, confusion, rape, incest, and countless other tragedies. It's all downstream, and churches have become recovery centers for people going over the falls and rapidly descending downstream."

The CEO sat forward in his chair. "What must happen," he said with emotion, "is for our children, the true leaders on earth, to go upstream. They must build and maintain the dam. Out of love, truth, discipline, and kindness they must take action."

"Where are the upstream people?" the Chairman demanded. "Just accepting us doesn't stop the downstream trends. People have to recognize what is going on and take personal action. We gave instructions on how to stay upstream, but for the most part, we've been ignored."

Barry usually allowed time to vent at the beginning of an interview in order to generate a free flow of conversation. Now it was time for him to probe deeper.

"People wonder why you don't step in and set things right," Barry commented.

The Chairman smiled. "Oh, we have all power and we see everything that is going on, but you must remember that we've stepped in many times in the past. Sure, it helps for a season, maybe a generation or two, but then they are back to where they started. Everything will be set right, with enormous and terrifying consequences when my Son triumphantly returns, but until then, what kind of life would it be if we controlled everything?"

The CEO noted, "We created man, we gave him the playbook, and we developed leaders or coaches who are supposed to recruit, train, and prepare. We expect the players to play and to win. They are the only ones allowed on the court. Sure, Satan lies and cheats and steals, but that's part of the game as well. We created the rules, we own the court, and we own the players, but they have forgotten how to play!"

"You can't walk on the court and take over the game," Barry said knowingly. "I see that. And I see that part of my job is to help these board members sort out their intentions and take the appropriate action."

"Yes," the CEO spoke up, "And since we are talking basketball, look at it this way: It's the fourth quarter, there isn't much time left, and they are behind."

"Exactly," said the Chairman, "and I'm the only one who knows how much time is left on the clock. Until then, we want all of the board members to see the light and fight upstream, to create that dam, and to love people like never before."

Barry restated the issues as he saw them, "It sounds like there needs to be a powerful movement of people with an understanding of your will and a commitment to making that happen."

"Well said," the Chairman stated, slapping the armrest on his chair.

The CEO looked at Barry for a second, then added, "Here's another way to look at it. Satan's lies are like a mind virus. He tried to tempt me in the desert, but I used the Word as my immunization. Most people, as you well know, are not strong in the Word. If they were aware of their dysfunctional belief systems, then they could take the antidote and avoid the virus. That's why we are starting with these top leaders. We can't make them change or do the work for them, but we are at least making them aware that life and freedom are available through you and our times together."

"It is easier to go downstream, which is why Satan thinks he's winning," Barry added, "but it is also possible to go upstream. We have eradicated polio, malaria, leprosy, and other sicknesses over a period of time by continually working to stem the tide. Offering solutions is always better than simply treating the symptoms."

"Right you are," stated the Chairman.

"The Word is the cure, the playbook, and the recipe for all things good," the CEO noted, "and if they went upstream, leading as we intended, then everyone would be impacted."

The Chairman elaborated, "Through what we are doing here with these leaders and their efforts, the truth will spread to the media, education, government, business, families, and the rest of the world. Starting a major movement begins by changing one person at a time."

Barry said, "I believe I am right in saying that the Great Commission should be the mission of all Christians. Christianity is losing market share because we are not bringing You to the world in a way that's producing positive results. I believe we need new methods to get to people without compromising the core message."

"Well said," commented the CEO. "Each person is unique, yet each person has the same commission."

The Chairman stated calmly, "When we meet next with the board, tell our leaders what we have discussed here. Long ago, we told them to be smart as vipers yet innocent as doves. This is a critical time for mankind. Let the movement begin at the next boardroom meeting."

15

The Final Board Meeting: The Movement Begins

Barry had worked all night refining, rethinking, and rehearsing for this meeting. The PowerPoint projector was set up and his presentation notes were ready. In front of each chair were neatly stacked reports with plastic covers.

Like a presiding judge, the Chairman ceremoniously entered from a side room, dressed in his robes, with the CEO walking at his side. They took their places at the head of the table.

Then, like a group of defendants, the twenty-five leaders filed in and took their seats in quiet anticipation of the most important board meeting ever.

The Chairman slowly rose to convene the meeting. He started, "Just to remind all of you that ninety days ago I asked the CEO to present the truth about your progress for our mission on earth. As you know, we are at thirty-two percent market share and declining. Other religions, even the 'none-of-the-above' group who don't claim any religion, are trying to decrease our market share."

He slowly looked around the room, then continued, "I don't need to repeat the same statistics of crime, alcoholism, violence, abortions, failed marriages, drug use, etc. The list goes on and on. This reflects three things: number one is the fact that people have rejected me and they are trying, and failing, to do things on their own. Number two is the fact that my people are ignoring the Great Commandment to love me, themselves, and others. And number three is the fact that my people have forgotten the Great Commission to go and make disciples of all nations.

"The loss in market share is why we called you together for an emergency board meeting. You are our key leaders on earth. So we asked you, with Barry's help, to find out what you can do to turn things around. The last boardroom meeting showed some progress, but we wanted to turn things up a notch."

Everyone was looking around, wondering what "turn things up a notch" might mean.

The Chairman went on, "As you know, your job is to lead the way, to lead the world to the foot of the cross, and to demonstrate just how much we love mankind. What has happened since our last meeting ... is that Barry had a face-to-face interview with Satan."

"Really?" someone blurted out.

"Is that possible?" another ventured.

"Why?" asked another.

"I knew you would have questions," the CEO said, standing beside the Chairman. "Barry's report is very interesting! If your eyes haven't been opened to what's happening around you, that report will do it. We want you to understand the seriousness of the situation."

The CEO motioned to Barry, "Would you please come up here? I'd like to also thank you for your efforts. I know many have deeply enjoyed working with you, and I'm sure many in this room have experienced a new way of looking at things, thanks to your work. It's been extremely helpful."

Barry walked up, stood at the corner of the table, and began, "I must say before we get started that it has been a pleasure working with you, and I look forward to a major transformation and turnaround of the company. It's up to you to make it happen. Are you up for the challenge?"

People nodded, and a few replied with a hearty, "Yes!"

"Very good, I knew you would," noted Barry. "But before I tell you about my interview with Satan — I know you are curious — I want to first bring your attention to some examples of transformation you have experienced yourselves during this project. You reached out and talked to former customers, a common practice for businesses, and you learned what attracts, retains, and/or loses business."

Barry pointed at Pastor Joe, sitting in one of the chairs around the table. "As you recall, Pastor Joe met with Halden Mack, a wounded recovering young soldier. He learned that young soldiers believe deeply in Jesus Christ because of the fear of death, but these same soldiers are totally disconnected from church and pastors. Pastor Joe was reminded of the basics of Jesus Christ: love, care, commitment, and kindness. Joe has changed his focus back to the basics. You heard his new perspective, how he was renewed and transformed."

"It's been incredible!" exclaimed Pastor Joe excitedly. "In fact, I have an email I received just this week from Halden Mack. Do you mind?"

Barry replied, "Sure. I'd love to see it."

Joe must have coordinated with the soundman, for suddenly the email appeared on the screen. It read:

Pastor Joe,

Thanks for meeting many of my buddies at the airport when they returned from Iraq and Afghanistan. And also for letting me speak at your church last week. We had over one hundred young men and women in uniforms. My mom and dad were so proud. Fred and Julie attended with their son Toby, who was stationed in Afghanistan. I look forward to working with you and others in your church to make sure we get it right for Jesus. — Hal

As the clapping died down, Barry continued, motioning toward Pastor Mike, "And Mike reconnected with John Carrington, a member who had left the church because of Pastor Mike's previous habits of control and ways of ostracizing those who didn't agree with him. Pastor Mike basically forced John and his wife Helen to quietly leave the church, and others followed. By reconnecting and listening to John, Mike exchanged his condescending attitude towards businesspeople for a powerful motivating role in helping encourage the creation of abundance under God. He also learned a great deal about stewardship in a business boardroom. He dropped his elitism and brought people together to work under God. Pastor Mike is learning to understand and work with businessmen in order to create unity and abundance, with the church as a catalyst."

"It has been tremendous!" Pastor Mike said, boldly and humbly. "John Carrington and I have started a Christian venture fund to show the world we can be strong Christians and ethically create abundance for all. We understand the concept of upstream versus downstream and instead of just giving away money from this venture, we will fund other ventures that will create value using Christian ethics. We want to multiply and create abundance in a way the world has never seen."

More clapping.

"Next we had Pastor George describe his meetings with Julie and Fred, a devoted couple from his church, and how they fiercely disagreed about how to handle issues, marriage counseling, and a rebellious daughter. Eventually Julie and Fred divorced, and their daughter Melinda went to jail. Pastor George was not convinced with their criticism of the church and his counseling program was warranted. He called for greater commitment from Julie and Fred and was reluctant to look deeper into his program and heart. However, as you remember, the Chairman chided him and questioned his motives and heart for people. George is not here today, which makes me think that you all agree his path was neither correct nor in line with the Chairman or CEO's plan."

Barry paused to take a sip of water. Only a few of the board members were looking around. Evidently they were the only ones who were surprised to hear that Pastor George was no longer on the team. Most already knew that George, under group pressure, had elected to resign.

"However, I'd like us all to reconsider Pastor George's fate. Here's an email I received from him."

On the screen flashed the email message:

> Barry,
>
> You will be delighted to hear that Fred and Julie have reconciled. It doesn't fix everything, but it is a start toward the family's healing.
>
> After you arranged for Pastor Joan to meet with Melinda, Joan called me to get more details on the situation. Then when I heard her report at the boardroom, I realized that she was coming from God's love, not dogma, rules, or a counseling process. What she said and has done has changed me. She forced me to raise my game.

> Pastor Joan and I met with Melinda, Fred, and Julie. I dropped all the counseling stuff and engaged from my heart with the love of Jesus. Everyone was ready to come together under love and submission, and their hearts melted, as did mine.
>
> So, I am asking, how can I help? I understand the board's reaction to my actions and statements, so I respectfully resigned. I pray for all of you. — Pastor George

Barry cleared his throat, then stated, "In all my years of consulting to boards, I have never asked for the board to reconsider a decision to remove someone. In this case, I've been touched by Pastor George's transformations, and based on the Kingdom principles of love, forgiveness, mercy, and repentance that I've seen in this boardroom, I respectfully and humbly ask the Chairman, the CEO, and the board to reconsider your decision to accept Pastor George's resignation."

The Chairman whispered to Barry, "Good move. I see transformation taking place in you as well." Then to the board, the Chairman stated, "I don't normally call for a vote, as that might start a dangerous precedent, but in this case, I'll ask for all in favor to stand."

There was a loud noise as all the chairs around the table were pushed back and everyone stood up.

"Please note that the vote is unanimous," exclaimed the Chairman.

The CEO added, "Pastor Joan, I think it would bring added healing to the situation if you and Barry were the ones to visit Pastor George personally and bring him back into the group."

Pastor Joan smiled, and Barry nodded. Both would willingly do this right away.

"Back to you, Barry," said the Chairman. "That was good."

"Thank you, and I agree," Barry replied, then kept going with the meeting. "The archbishop was a dramatic example of the transformation power of feedback from others who care, whether they share all your beliefs or not. Beliefs are supposed to be helpful, but they can also be destructive or counterproductive. Jack, a former priest, met with the archbishop and challenged his role in, among other things, protecting pedophile priests. The archbishop realized that there was no substitute for a strong relationship with Jesus. The archbishop displayed his new life by making vows in this very boardroom, by taking action to reveal pedophile priests, and by serving God first and foremost."

The room again erupted in spontaneous applause. The archbishop flushed red and smiled back at everyone else in the room. Barry knew the response from the team meant more to the archbishop than anyone else would ever know.

The archbishop rose and spoke. "Jack and I had the opportunity to meet with the cardinal last week and share our new commitment to Jesus. The cardinal was overwhelmed. We're starting a group to help all Christians come together under the simple good news of Christ. Jack and I are also starting a program for the clergy who molested the children. They need help. We are working to get past our own resistance to forgiveness. It is, without question, an upstream project."

"We heard from Pastor Joan," Barry continued. "Her love and unity took things to a whole new level of service and commitment. I could see that many of you were touched by what she said. I also know that all of you were challenged by her choices and actions as she worked with Melinda. I am pleased to report that just yesterday, Melinda chose to put her faith in Jesus Christ based on the love from everyone. She is hungry to understand how the Bible teaches us to live more effective lives. I am confident that her future is going to be very different than her past."

Again, the room broke into applause, with Pastor Joan clapping along with the rest of them. For the first time, both the Chairman and CEO were also clapping.

Pastor Joan raised her hand, and after Barry acknowledged her, she said, "I must admit that at first I thought Barry was just another male chauvinist trying to criticize women. Boy was I wrong. He forced me to go beyond stereotypes for men and women and to stretch my perspective. This lifted up the vision for all of us in the boardroom to go beyond our petty egos and causes and to see the truth and move forward together. I was amazed how everyone experienced transformation and saw major changes in others, which is only a God thing. I am also proud to be part of this group and the decision to reach out again to Pastor George. As we reconcile our differences and reach out to the world, the impact will be massive."

There was a mixture of laughing and clapping when Joan finished.

Barry moved briefly through the interviews he had with the other members around the table, highlighting the transformation and breakthrough that had occurred. All the members were evidently unified and excited about what they had learned, both individually and collectively, since the first board meeting had been called.

"On that note, I want to shift gears and discuss my interview with Satan," Barry explained, as he looked around the room. It suddenly got quiet. "In your packet you'll find a section entitled, 'Satan's Strategy to Destroy Christianity.' I didn't just make it up, in case you are wondering. What you will read is powerful and telling, but I'll let you read it on your own later. I have heard it said that many Christian leaders do not believe in a literal existence of Satan. If that is the case, and since Satan is fully described in the Bible as a real entity, how can you not believe in his existence? Can someone explain this to me?"

The archbishop stood, straightened his robes, and spoke, "The Roman Catholic church over the years has changed its position on Satan. We used to practice exorcism to rid individuals of demons and Satan, but now we consider it mental illness, not possession."

"Yes, that's certainly more politically correct," Barry commented. "Anyone else?"

Pastor Mike put his hand up. Barry nodded toward him, and Mike began, "I think Christians believe in Satan, but more in a figurative sense rather than as a real individual prowling the earth looking to devour the unwary. He is a concept rather than a reality. People don't want to be ridiculed by describing a guy in a red suit with horns and a tail running around causing problems. We're all much more sophisticated today. Science has explained a lot that used to be superstition."

Barry asked, "But if people believe there is no Satan, will they believe there is a hell? And if people question the existence of hell, the natural next step is to question if heaven is real either."

The board members weren't entirely sure what to say.

Before things deteriorated into an open argument around the room, Barry added, "Look, I can tell you are divided; that much is evident. But it is a division that we have to address if we are going to take things to the next level. Personally, I have a hard time believing that Christians would question the reality of Satan, but that was one of the primary reasons for our interview."

The Chairman leaned forward in his chair and simply stated, "When you acknowledge that he is real, you will naturally care much more about what he is doing."

There was a silence in the room as the board members digested the truth of those words.

"We are obviously not on the same page here," Pastor Mike volunteered, speaking up for the rest of the leaders, "and we need to be if we are going to work toward the common goal of regaining market share."

Barry pointed out, "I can't help but wonder how it is that denominations present such different interpretations of Satan and hell. Compound that with the question of what it means to be saved. Is it by faith, grace, works, or alliance to the church?"

"No wonder we are losing market share," someone spoke up from the end of the table.

Another board member stood up. Barry had interviewed him over the phone multiple times, but the man lived in England, so they had not been able to meet face to face. "I have a big contingent in my church of hard-working, wealthy, self-sustaining, educated people who will say, 'How can Satan think we are so stupid and mindless to be manipulated by a shadowy figure who plants ideas into our heads?' They will feel it's insulting to think that they are being controlled."

"Good questions," Barry said. "The best way to answer a question is sometimes to ask further questions. I prepared these questions for all of you to consider, but now that I think about it, you might want to take these questions back to your people."

Barry pointed to the white screen and quickly took them through several questions:

- **Disunity**: Is it an accident that there are hundreds of denominations that can't agree on doctrine?.

- **Adversarial**: How do you explain a culture that pits us against each other? Women vs. men, children vs. parents, rich vs. poor, conservatives vs. liberal, religion vs. secular, and more.

- **Selfishness:** What about the breakup of families over "irreconcilable differences"?

- **Sickness:** Why would a civilized country need to kill so many unborn children every day?

- **Following:** Why do we willingly accept all the latest trends, crazes, crushes, and habits that society throws our way instead of leading the way toward what is right?

- **Loveless:** Why do people forget to love one another?

Barry clicked through the last bullet point, then turned to the table and said, "Personally, I think that Satan's strategy of staying covert, creating distractions, causing resentment among groups, and appealing to people's rationalizations to get what they want seems to be working incredibly well, don't you?"

The archbishop stood. "If I might add a little to what you've said? To those who don't believe in a literal devil, how can you deny the evilness of protecting pedophiles? That's not God's will. And cover-ups to save the church, that's not pure and holy. Did we succumb to wanting to be politically correct under pressure to conform to the culture? Are some churches allowing the foundation of marriage to change because it's actually a good thing for families or for the church? Is promoting total freedom a good move for the unborn child? If people in the church are insulted by the idea that Satan is using them, then I think we as the leaders should be mortified that we fell for it."

Stacking his papers in a pile, Barry was about to speak when another pastor stood up and said, "I agree with the archbishop, and though I might lose my head for saying this, I've often wondered what would happen if we were to unite as one denomination. I mean, wouldn't that be a powerful witness of our unity? But that may be a can of worms that is best left unopened … I don't know. I think the most important question to ask ourselves is, 'How we can take God's love and life-changing power out to the world.'"

There were several heads nodding in agreement, most likely to the second part of what the pastor said.

The soundman, again way ahead of the curve, flashed these words across the screen:

#1 — Take God's love and life-changing power
out to the world.

Barry commented, "I like that. Thank you. It is indeed all about taking 'God's love and life-changing power out to the world.' I think that phrase could be our motto, our rallying cry. What do you say?"

The CEO and Chairman smiled, and there was a hearty chorus of "yes" answers and a lot of clapping from the board members.

Walking back to his leather chair, Barry sat down and said, "Okay, with everything that we've discussed today and looking at the transformation that has taken place in each of your lives and in all that we have learned together, it is time to outline the next steps. These next steps are the specific action steps that will take each and every one of us to the next level. This phase is what I do with every company I work with, and the results are phenomenal because the entire team is functioning as one unit."

They were visibly excited about that!

"You will be surprised at the rate of progress, not because you never did it before, but because you are all united with one common plan," Barry explained. "I suggest a sample plan for everyone based on the lessons we have learned."

On the screen flashed these bullet points:

- Develop a simple, loving message based on the Bible.

- Learn and implement Kingdom principles.

- Give people the opportunity to accept Jesus as their Lord.

- Encourage personal relationships with Jesus Christ.

"The next step is to outline the specifics that will include time frames, assignments, and clear goals," related Barry, gearing up for the final part of his presentation.

The Chairman, leaning forward and putting his hands on the edge of the table, interrupted, "This is it. This is where the movement begins!"

Everyone looked to the Chairman. He scanned the faces around the table, looking into each pair of eyes, and continued, "I am pleased with all of you and have enjoyed seeing transformation take place in each of your lives. I recognize at this point that it is Barry's job to condense everything into five easy steps, but I'm not going to let him do that."

Barry was as surprised as everyone else. He was also about to speak when the CEO suddenly stood up.

"This meeting is now complete," the CEO stated with kindness and finality. "You all have the same mission ... how you walk it out is as unique as you are. Be transformed and take God's love and life-changing power out to the world."

Let the movement begin!

To participate in the movement, check us out on
www.Facebook.com/GodintheBoardroom

"But seek first his kingdom and his righteousness, and all these things will be given to you as well."
— Matthew 6:33 (NIV)

About the Authors

Larry Cabaldon, CEO of the Boardroom Performance Group, consults at the board of directors level for public companies, financial institutions, non-profit, government, private companies, and ministries. He has assessed hundreds of executives and dozens of boards on behalf of investors, regulators, acquirers, directors, CEOs, and stakeholders in order to improve organizational performance. He utilizes his international executive search background and corporate governance experience to help companies in crisis or organizations that want to move to the next level.

Several years ago, when Larry understood his role in the Great Commission, he and his wife Pat developed www.myjesusplan.com to help people explore their spirituality and develop a stronger relationship with God. The classes were originally designed for adults and MBA students at a major Christian school. It had a broader appeal to everyone, non-Christians and Christians alike, because it gave them the opportunity to explore their own spiritually without pressure from pastors, teachers, or parents. Young people were very concerned about their relationship with God and others but did not have a way of exploring that with others. Now they do with their own MyJesusPlan.

To stay updated, visit www.MyJesusPlan.com

Brian Klemmer is a graduate of the United States Military Academy, a best-selling author, and a riveting, unforgettable speaker and seminar leader. His company, Klemmer & Associates Leadership Seminars, Inc., has fourteen facilitators who have worked with hundreds of thousands of people throughout the world, helping them produce measurable and long-lasting changes in their lives. His clients include Aetna Life Insurance, American Suzuki Corporation, General Electric, Walt

Disney Attractions, and a dozen network-marketing and direct-sales companies.

Brian has studied leadership since graduating from the United States Military Academy (1968-1972). He's the author of several best selling books, such as the *Compassionate Samurai* (a number one business book of 2008), and including others such as *If How-To's Were Enough, We Would All Be Skinny, Rich, & Happy*; *When Good Intentions Run Smack into Reality*; and *Eating the Elephant One Bite at a Time*. Known for his humorous and practical style of communicating, Brian is one of today's most in-demand speakers.

Brian also regularly speaks in churches on practical applications of kingdom principles and does transformation retreats for large church staffs.

For more information and to receive a powerful leadership lesson with illustration and action item for the week free, go to www.klemmer.com and click on the FREE OFFER.

Thoughts/Notes/Revelations:

Thoughts/Notes/Revelations:

Thoughts/Notes/Revelations: